S.T.E.A.L.T.H.
ACCESS
DENIED

S.T.E.A.L.T.H.
ACCESS DENIED

JASON ROHAN

nosy
crow

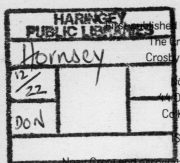
First published in the UK in 2022 by Nosy Crow Ltd
The Crow's Nest, 14 Baden Place
Crosby Row, London, SE1 1YW, UK

Nosy Crow Eireann Ltd
44 Orchard Grove, Kenmare,
Co. Kerry, V93 FY22, Ireland

ISBN: 978 1 83994 338 6

Nosy Crow and associated logos are trademarks and/or registered
trademarks of Nosy Crow Ltd

Printed and bound in the UK by Clays Ltd, Elcograf S.p.A.
Typeset by Tiger Media

Papers used by Nosy Crow are made from wood grown in sustainable
forests

MIX
Paper from
responsible sources
FSC® C018072

3 5 7 9 10 8 6 4 2

www.nosycrow.com

To Dominik, Ben and Jacob,
the original S.T.E.A.L.T.H. team members

08:52

"Why are there police at your house?"

Arun blinked in response, unable to decide which was more weird: what Donna had said, or that she had spoken to him at all.

"Wuh?" was the best he could manage.

Donna gripped the lapel of his school blazer and hauled him aside. Other Year Sevens surged past in the corridor, hurrying to their classrooms for registration.

"I said, why are the feds at your house, dummy? I saw them show up just after you left."

Arun shook his head, dumbfounded. "I don't know what you're talking about."

"That's right, Donna," Sam said, sticking up for his best friend.

"How would you know?" Donna sneered.

"Let me go," Arun said, trying to pull away. "We'll be late for registration." The corridor was almost clear.

"Listen," Donna said, "you can go to class and be teacher's pet, or you can come with me and suss what's going on. They were plain-clothes cops, you know."

"How would *you* know that?" Sam said.

"Because I know," Donna said. She stormed off towards the stairs to the playground. "You coming?"

The two boys looked at each other for a moment, before Arun shrugged and trotted after her.

Sam stared, watching his friend disappear down the stairs. He could hardly believe it: Arun had ditched him – for a girl too. Then again, what if Donna was right and the police really were at Arun's house?

"Hey, wait for me!" he said, and hurried to catch up.

"Follow me," Donna said. "Do what I do, walk where I walk. Just don't run – that's a dead giveaway."

Donna led the way out of the Most Sacred Heart High School with practised ease, guiding the boys past the bicycle racks, round the sports hall and across the grass to the main gates, making sure to keep the hedges between them and the school building, before slipping out into the street.

Arun said nothing. Everyone knew Donna skipped classes; he just never expected to be joining her.

"Why would the police be at my house?" Arun said, giving in to curiosity.

"Beats me." Donna shrugged. "Maybe your dad's jacked

a bank or something."

"Ha!" Sam scoffed. "More like *your* da— *Oof!*"

Donna's fist disappeared into his middle before he could finish. Sam doubled over and sagged to his knees, holding his wounded belly.

"You take that back! You take that back right now!" Donna shouted, standing over him.

"Can you two keep it down?" Arun said, helping Sam to straighten up. "We're in enough trouble already, skipping class, without telling the whole street we're here."

"She punched me!" Sam wailed.

"And you deserved it," Arun said, ignoring the scandalised look on Sam's face. "Now say sorry and let's go."

Donna stood with her arms folded, jaw thrust out, and glared at Sam. He looked to Arun for help but his friend's mind was elsewhere.

"All right. I'm sorry," Sam mumbled.

Donna sucked her teeth and said, "Man, why am I even bothering to help a couple of losers like you?" She marched towards the main road.

Arun hesitated, waiting for Sam to move.

"I thought we were friends," Sam said.

"We are," Arun said. "It's just – if she's right, I have to know what's going on. I can't wait until school's finished.

You'd be the same."

"Yeah, I suppose."

The two boys ran after the departing girl. They had almost caught her up, when a man's voice from behind bellowed, "You kids, stay where you are!"

Arun and Sam looked back to see a slab of muscle marching towards them from the direction of the school. "I've found the brat," the lump said into his phone. "I'll bring him in."

"Who's that?" Sam asked.

"I don't know," Arun replied with a shrug. "Doesn't look like a teacher."

The brute reached them, checked the phone in his hand and said to Arun, "You're Arun Lal, right?"

"Maybe," Arun said, unsure if it was meant as a question or a statement.

"You need to come with me. Just you."

"I've only just left the school grounds," Arun protested. "It's hardly truanting."

"I don't care about truanting. This is for your own safety. Now I won't tell you again," the bruiser said. "Come with me – or else."

"Who are you?" Donna asked. She came closer, pushing a frizzy lock of hair behind her ear while keeping her other hand pressed firmly in her blazer pocket.

"Police. This boy's under arrest."

Donna tilted her head. "On what charge?"

"Littering. Trespass. Who cares? I don't answer to you."

"My mum's a lawyer," Donna said. "I know my rights."

"Yeah? Well, why don't you just wind your neck in, or I'll arrest you too?"

Donna's eyes narrowed. "I want to see your warrant card."

The man glanced around to check the street was clear, before unbuttoning his jacket.

"Right here," he said, drawing it back to reveal an automatic pistol in a shoulder holster. "Now, bog off before things really get nast— *AaAAGH!*"

It was only from the corner of his eye, but Arun saw Donna's hand whip up from her pocket, heard the *pfft-pfft* of a spray bottle, and the next thing he knew the big man was doubled over with his hands covering his face, shrieking, "My eyes! My eyes!" His phone lay on the pavement at Arun's feet.

"Don't just stand there, you idiots!" Donna yelled. "Run!"

Arun snatched up the phone and tore down the road after her.

09:16

Donna, Arun and Sam raced round another corner and ducked into a front garden bordered by a tall hedge. Sam sank down, clutching the stitch in his side and heaving in great lungfuls of air.

Arun finally looked at the phone in his hand. "No way."

Smiling up at him was his own face, only a few years younger and holding an enormous ice cream.

"What's that about?" Sam asked, peering over his shoulder. "Why's that bloke got your picture on his phone?"

Donna ducked her head round the hedge and kneeled on the grass. "No sign of him," she panted. "Reckon we ditched him."

"Who was that?" Arun said, putting the phone away. "And what did you do to him?"

Donna pulled a scuffed hair conditioner bottle from her blazer pocket. "Home-made pepper spray," she said. "My own recipe. Mash up some Trini Scorpion peppers, mix 'em with my grandma's pickle, strain off the juice, and – major licks. It's good on burgers too."

Arun was incredulous. "You carry that stuff around? Why?"

Donna shrugged. "Never know when you'll need it."

"That was awesome!" Sam said.

Donna ignored him. "What was that geezer up to anyway?" she said to Arun. "Was he trying to … kidnap you?"

Arun snorted. "No! He must've been from the school or something."

Donna cuffed him round the head. "Hello? Duh! He had a gun, you doughnut. If he's a copper, then I'm Beyoncé. Man, I can't believe you're supposed to be clever." She rose to her feet. "Come on, let's go see what the real Five-O are doing at your place."

As they approached Arun's house at 23 Mitchell Drive, Donna ducked down and indicated a silver Audi Q5, parked outside.

"See? Told you," she said. "Unmarked police car."

"How can you tell?" Sam asked.

"Because I can," Donna said. "Alloy wheels, extra mirrors, plain plates – it's all there."

"Hmm … assuming you're right," Arun said, sounding unconvinced, "what now?"

Donna shrugged. "I am right. It's your house. How do we get in?"

"What, besides ringing the doorbell and saying 'Hello, Mum, I bunked off school' in front of two police officers?"

He paused, thought for a moment, then added, "The back door's usually unlocked when Mum's at home."

"Let's roll then. After you."

Still crouched down, Arun led the way on to the drive, through the side gate and round to the rear of the house. They huddled in the shadows, with the back garden stretched out before them. A bench outside the kitchen extension was shaded by the overhang. The door to the utility room was slightly ajar.

"Now what?" Sam whispered.

"We have to get close enough to listen in and see why Arun's mum's getting nicked," Donna explained with exaggerated patience.

Arun glared at her. "My mum's not getting arrested. It's probably just a mistake, or something she witnessed."

"Hello? Plain-clothes detectives? Duh!"

"You'd know all about that," Sam said.

"Do I have to punch you again?"

"Will you two stop arguing?" Arun said. "What we need is a diversion..."

His eyes lit upon the bird table and he smiled.

Inside Arun's house, Detective Inspector Andrew Moss perched on the sofa, cradling a cup of milky tea, now cold. His partner, Detective Constable Sunny Patel, sat opposite, her notebook in hand.

Arun's mother, Heidi, sat between them, her hands clasped tightly. No one spoke. *TOCK-TOCK-TOCK*. The only sound was the mantelpiece clock counting the seconds – which was why DI Moss jumped at the sudden blare of a car alarm and spilt tea on to his lap. *BEEP-BEEP-BEEP!* He ran to the front door to see who was stupid enough to try stealing an unmarked police car, while DC Patel and Mrs Lal rushed to the window.

Moss was just in time to see a flash of amber leap from the roof of the car and bolt for the safety of the nearest tree, flying up the trunk. Scowling, he wandered out to the car and saw that someone had scattered bird seed on the roof. He swore under his breath, brushed it clean and went back into the house.

Upstairs, the three children stayed low on the landing, listening intently for voices from the living room.

"I can't believe that worked!" Donna whispered, and

gave Arun a congratulatory thump on the arm.

He put a finger to his lips and they heard the front door close as DI Moss returned.

"What was it?" DC Patel asked. "Is the alarm playing up again?" She handed Moss a paper towel to dab the tea stain.

"No. A stupid cat chasing some birds jumped on the car and set off the alarm."

"That would be next door's ginger tom," Arun's mother said. "Horrible pest, always pooping in our yard."

Silence returned, before Heidi finally said, "What happens now? This waiting around is killing me."

"You have to be patient, Mrs Lal." It was Patel's voice, soothing and reassuring. "We have a specialist team on the way from MI6; they're trained to deal with kidnappings. Your husband is going to be just fine."

Listening from the upstairs landing, Donna's eyes were wide as she stared at Arun. "No freaking way! Someone's kidnapped your dad!"

09:35

Crouched upstairs on the landing, Sam poked Arun in the ribs. "Did she say 'MI6'? That's British secret service. You know ... James Bond stuff," he whispered.

Donna leaned closer to Arun and hissed, "This is madness! I thought your dad was just some dry old banker."

"So did I," Arun said.

Outside, two black Range Rovers pulled up and eight men stepped out, all dressed in black suits and dark sunglasses. Only the colour of their ties differed.

BING-BONG! DI Moss sprang to answer the doorbell.

Donna put a finger to her lips and leaned forward to listen to the voices in the hall.

"Inspector Moss?" a gravelly voice said. "You can call me Quinn. My team will handle things from here. Your babysitting duties are done. You're free to go."

"If you don't mind, Mr Quinn, we'd like to stay. You know, take some notes, learn from the best," Moss said.

"Actually, I do mind, but flattery is good. You can stay on

two conditions: one, keep your gob shut; and two, stay out of my way. Deal?"

"Deal."

Donna turned towards the boys with both eyebrows raised, as the clumping of feet made its way into the living room.

"Mrs Lal?" Quinn said, extending his hand. "Or may I call you Heidi? The name's Quinn, from British Intelligence. Can I ask what you know of your husband's job?"

"I-I don't see why that..." Arun's mum hesitated. "Krishan works for the government. He's an analyst at the Bank of England."

Quinn grunted. "Is he now? This morning, on the way to work, his car was involved in a minor traffic accident. I'd like you to take a look at this." He handed her an iPad. "This is CCTV footage taken from around Chelsea Bridge at seven fifty-seven this morning," Quinn said. "You can see your husband's BMW coming into frame now. He stops here at the red light."

Listening from upstairs, Arun closed his eyes and tried to picture the scene.

Quinn continued. "Watch. As soon as the light goes green and he starts to roll – *BANG!* – he gets T-boned, right here, by a black Volvo V90 that jumps the light."

The black-and-white footage was silent but it was easy to imagine the screeching of tyres, followed by the crunch of metal against metal and the pattering of glass on tarmac.

Arun's mum watched through her fingers.

"If you go back, pause and zoom in, you can see the airbag inflating, so we're pretty sure Krishan wasn't hurt, just shaken up a bit. And now, if I let it go on, you'll see that here, about twenty seconds later, an ambulance pulls up and takes your husband away."

"Mr Quinn ... are you saying that this ... accident ... was deliberate?" Heidi said. "A set-up?"

"Exactly." Quinn nodded. "Now, the London Ambulance Service does like to brag about improved response times but twenty seconds, in rush-hour traffic, is some going." He cleared his throat. "The Volvo had false registration plates, as did the ambulance. Witnesses report Krishan being pulled unconscious from his car by two paramedics who chucked him into the ambulance. This was at seven fifty-nine this morning, and no one has seen or heard from your husband since."

Heidi covered her mouth with her hand.

"Now, think carefully," Quinn said. "Do you know anyone

who could be harbouring a grudge against your husband? Anyone at all?"

Heidi shook her head, blinking back tears. "No. Krishan was – is – well liked by everyone. He's thoughtful, considerate, remembers everyone's birthdays, never has a bad word to say."

Quinn sighed. "That's what I was afraid of. So, if it isn't anything personal, it has to be professional." He turned to one of his agents who wore an emerald tie. "Green, get the prime minister's office on the phone. Now."

Upstairs, Sam stifled a groan and kicked his leg out.

"Shhh!" Donna hissed.

Sam winced. "It's cramp! I can't help it."

Quinn froze, looking up at the ceiling. "Mrs Lal, is there anyone else at home?"

"No. Arun ... my son, is at school."

Quinn's gaze swung back to Heidi. "Then what was that noise? Brown, go and check it out."

Brown reached into his jacket and drew a Glock 37 automatic pistol. Once in the hall, he screwed a silencer on to the barrel and moved for the stairs.

09:52

Donna's eyes were wide. "Someone's coming!"

"This way!" Arun whispered, shuffling silently across the carpeted landing towards his parents' room.

Brown's soft footsteps on the stairs were getting closer. Arun counted them: he knew there were thirteen steps; a tiny creak meant Brown was on number six.

Donna and Sam crawled after him into the front bedroom. Inside was a double bed with four decorative cushions propped up against the pillows, a dresser, bedside cabinets and fitted wardrobes along the wall.

"Under the bed," Arun hissed.

Donna hit the floor and shimmied under.

"We won't all fit," Sam said, judging the space.

"You're right," Arun agreed. "Get in the wardrobe – quick!"

Brown reached the landing, and cocked his head to listen. He could have sworn he'd heard faint whispers but maybe he'd imagined it. Four doors led off the landing, all closed.

He went to the nearest on his immediate left. Pressing

his back against the wall, he pushed the door open and sent his pistol muzzle ahead to sweep the room. He peered in to see a toilet and washbasin. One junior toothbrush stood in a Spider-Man cup by the sink. The boy's bathroom, Brown surmised, stepping out again.

He opened the opposite door, which led into a bedroom with an elevated single bunk bed and a desk underneath, which had a crate full of electronic circuitry beside it. A half-built quadcopter drone rested on a chest of drawers, the remaining parts laid out beside it, and a high-powered telescope stood on a tripod by the window.

Two doors remained. Brown tried the door on the far side of the landing, furthest from the stairs. The room beyond was small, neat and centred around a cluttered desk with a flat-screen monitor and laptop docking station sitting on it. Bookcases lined three walls crammed with all manner of texts – classics, fantasies, thrillers, advanced mathematics textbooks, souvenir football programmes, *National Geographic* magazines, graphic novels. Pride of place on the remaining wall went to a signed Newcastle United football shirt mounted in a glass case, with a large number of framed certificates and diplomas around it. Krishan Lal's study, Brown decided, which meant the last door must be the master bedroom.

His black-gloved hand reached for the door.

Inside the bedroom, hidden amid the shoes and dust under the bed, Arun and Donna were listening to Brown's movements, tracking his path from room to room.

"Here he comes," Arun whispered as the door handle began to turn.

Donna's eyes lit up as an idea struck her. "What's your home number?" she asked Arun.

"Huh?"

"Your home phone number? What is it?"

The door opened and they could see a pair of black shoes enter the room. The children held their breath, not daring to make a sound.

Donna reached for her smartphone and waved it in front of Arun's face.

The feet walked up to the bed and stopped.

Arun shut his eyes tightly, willing the shoes to walk away. They didn't. Donna prodded him and he opened his eyes to see the feet pacing slowly round the bed, towards the adjoining bathroom.

Arun started keying numbers into Donna's phone and the digits appeared mutely.

Brown finished checking the en-suite bathroom and

was about to leave when he thought he heard a sound from inside one of the wardrobe units. He levelled the pistol and reached for the handle.

Inside, Sam held his breath and shrank back, burrowing under a folded duvet.

Downstairs, the house phone rang.

"That'll be the kidnappers making contact," Quinn barked. "Everyone get ready. Heidi, let it ring six times and then keep them talking as long as you can. Brown! Get down here, now!"

Brown hesitated, his hand poised on the wardrobe door, then hurried out of the room and back down the stairs. Donna counted five rings and ended the call.

Just as Heidi reached for the phone, the ringing stopped, amid a chorus of groans and curses.

Arun slowly exhaled and let his forehead rest on the floor. Donna grinned and kissed her phone.

Her smile vanished as Quinn's growl carried upstairs: "Get me an immediate trace on that call. I want to know who it was from and where they are. Move!"

10:12

Downstairs, in the living room, Agent Green lowered his phone.

"Gaffer, we have a positive ID," he said to Quinn. "That call came from a pay-as-you-go phone registered to a Miss Donna Critchlow. Aged twelve."

"Twelve?" Quinn looked to Heidi. "You know her?"

Heidi shook her head slowly. "There's a Donna Critchlow in Arun's class... I know her mother from the playground... Very nice lady... She's a lawyer in the City, but Arun has never really talked about Donna."

"So why would she be calling here?" Quinn mused.

"Wrong number?" Heidi suggested.

"Or maybe Arun has a secret girlfriend?" Brown said with a raised eyebrow.

"He's twelve!" Heidi said.

Brown shrugged. "You never know with kids these days."

Quinn's eyes narrowed. "Let's run a background check on her, just in case."

"What are you thinking, boss?" Brown asked.

Quinn pursed his lips. "It may be nothing. It's just … in cases like this, nothing happens by accident."

Upstairs, on the landing, Sam was scowling. "Ooh, these guys are good," he whispered. "I didn't think you could trace a pre-pay mobile that quickly."

"They're not that clever if they think I'm your girlfriend," Donna muttered, elbowing Arun.

"Hey!" Arun complained. "Why is it that *he* says it and you hit *me*? Go and hit him if you're so hard."

The house phone rang.

In the living room Quinn held up his hand and counted off six rings before jabbing a finger towards Arun's mum.

She picked up the phone, trying to sound as calm as possible. "Hello? Lal residence."

"Hello? Heidi? It's Galahad, from Krishan's office." The caller's clipped tones echoed from a loudspeaker connected to the call-tracing equipment Quinn's team had set up. "Is everything OK?"

"Galahad! Yes – yes, everything's fine. Just a busy morning here, that's all."

"I know the feeling. Is Krishan still there?"

"No. He left a while ago."

"Oh. He's running late. That's not like him. Must've had a flat tyre or something... Listen, I, uh, have a tiny favour to ask, if you don't mind. You know Krishan and I have this big presentation we're supposed to be doing today for all the top brass...?"

"Yes, he mentioned something about it. A new software release?"

"Yes, that's the one. Well, I have my half of the presentation here but Krishan didn't send me his half, so I'm wondering if it's still on his laptop and, since he's not here yet, I was, er, wondering..."

"What?"

"If he might have a copy at home? An earlier draft or something? I mean, without his half I'm snookered. The whole thing goes belly up."

Heidi's face reddened and her knuckles turned white as she gripped the receiver. "Galahad, it's just software. You can always do your presentation another day. It's hardly life and death, is it?"

"No, no. You're quite right. That's stupid of me. Sorry. I'm so stressed about this thing that I'm not thinking straight. Krishan did take his laptop with him, though, this morning? He didn't leave it behind, did he?"

"Galahad, I really have more important things to think

about right now than your blooming presentation! If it's any help, Kris didn't bring his laptop home on Friday at all. It was our anniversary and I told him that he had to leave work at work and he wasn't to do any bank stuff at home, so he left the laptop behind. It's probably in the safe in his office or somewhere like that. I'm sure you can find it and do what you need to with it."

"Heidi, you're a star. Krishan's so lucky to have you. Thank you, thank you, thank you. You've saved my life."

"Always a pleasure, Galahad," she said coldly. "Talk to you soon."

"Thanks, Heidi."

"Oh, and good luck with your presentation. Tell Kris to call me when he gets in."

"Hm? Oh, yes. Yes, I'll tell him. Bye."

Green switched off the recording equipment.

"Who was that moron?" Quinn spat in disgust. "Colleague gets kidnapped and all he cares about is his stupid presentation?"

DI Moss smiled. "He's not been officially reported as missing yet."

Quinn stopped, mid-rant. "Good point, well made. Weren't you supposed to be keeping quiet?" He stared out of the window for a moment. "Right. Looks like we're going to be here a while then. One of you boys, put the kettle on. Heidi, who was that twit on the phone?"

Back on the landing, Arun shifted his weight and propped himself up on one elbow, a puzzled look on his face.

"What's the matter?" Sam asked. "Other than the obvious?"

"Something doesn't sound right," Arun whispered. "Galahad's been Dad's workmate for years. If they're doing a presentation together, why didn't Dad just email it to him when it was done? It's not like he was working on it over the weekend or anything. They were both in the office on Friday, and it must have been finished by then, so why not just give him a copy?"

"You think he was lying?" Sam said. "Why?"

Arun pulled the phone he'd picked up from his pocket and stared at it.

"I'll tell you what *I* thought was weird," Donna said to Arun. "Right at the end, when your mum said for your dad to call her when he got in, that Galahad man ... he sounded like he wasn't expecting your dad to come in at all."

"I remember this," Arun said, his eyes still fixed on the phone. "That photo of me was from a company picnic three years ago. Galahad took it. How did it end up in the hands of that thug?"

Sam's mind was working furiously. "All right, assuming just for a second … what would that Galahad bloke want by phoning your mum? Like she said, he can just postpone his presentation. What's the big deal?"

"Dad's laptop," Arun said quietly. "That's what he was really after. The presentation was just a decoy."

"You think so? What's so special about this laptop?" Sam asked.

Arun's eyes narrowed and his jaw tightened. "I don't know. Let's go and find out."

10:36

"I thought your mum said the laptop was still at work," Sam whispered, as he followed Arun and Donna into the study.

"It is, but my dad backs everything up on a second computer just in case. He keeps it in here."

Donna looked around the study. "Is that shirt real?" she said, eyeing the striped football jersey in its case.

"Yeah, Dad won it in a charity auction. He's a big football nut."

"Should we be doing this? I mean, we're in enough trouble already." Sam looked at the door, as if expecting it to open at any moment.

"What's the alternative?" Arun said. "Hang around on the landing and hope no one comes up for a wee?"

He moved round the large desk and slid the swivel chair aside. Six drawers faced him, three on each side. He reached for the handle of the bottom-right drawer and pulled, but nothing happened.

"It's locked," he said. "So much for that idea."

"Can we break it open?" Sam asked.

"Not without making a ton of noise."

Sam slumped down. "Now what do we do? Is there a key?"

Donna pushed past him and made her way round the desk.

"Let me see it," she said, kneeling by the drawers. A small keyhole glinted on the right, just under the desk top. Donna reached up for the stationery tray and selected a black pen, a hole punch and a paper clip.

"Gimme some space," she said to Arun, who crept out of her way.

He and Sam both watched as Donna straightened out one end of the paper clip, carefully put the long end into the hole punch, positioning it below one of the bladed cylinders, and squeezed the lever arm gently, shaving off an edge and flattening the tiny metal rod. She took it out and inspected it.

She then snapped the metal clip off the pen cap. With the flat end of the clip pushed into the bottom half of the keyhole, she turned the cylinder clockwise as far as it would go. With her other hand she poked the flat end of the paper clip into the top part of the keyhole, moving it in and out slowly, pushing up the locking pins inside while holding the cylinder tight.

"Wow. If you concentrated in class like that…" Sam said.

There was a click and the lock turned.

"You did it!" Arun said.

Donna smiled. "You doubted?"

Sam looked at her, his eyes wide. "How do you know all this stuff?"

"What? You think just cos I'm not top of the class like you that means I don't know things?"

"No, that's not what I meant. It's just … you're … cool."

Donna rolled her eyes, but couldn't hide the smile breaking across her face, so she turned away. "Right, man, where's this laptop?"

Arun opened the bottom drawer and took out a sleek black computer. He lifted the lid and pushed the power button.

The three children crowded round and watched the screen blink into life. A message appeared: *Place fingertip on scanner to initiate Login.*

Sam groaned. "A fingerprint reader? Nooo."

Arun thought for a few seconds. "Sam, you're the expert. How do these things work?"

Sam ran a pudgy hand through his fair hair. "It depends on the type of scanner. Some only look for ridges, others check for a pulse too. The really clever ones scan in 3D."

"Which type is this? Can you tell by looking?"

Sam shrugged, and picked up the laptop. He peered closely at the small sensor pad in the bottom-right corner. "I can see a faint red light, like you get with an optical mouse ... so I'd say it just wants a pattern to read."

Arun grinned. "Then I have an idea," he said. "Back in a minute." He crept out of the study.

Downstairs, in the living room, Agent Green was scowling at a message on his phone.

"Gaffer, that Critchlow girl you were asking about... She's got a criminal record."

DI Moss, perched by the door and trying to remain unnoticed, straightened up.

"At twelve? What's she done?" Quinn growled. "Tried selling her granny on eBay?"

"Minor stuff," Green said, reading from the email. "Trespass, truancy, vandalism, computer misuse, littering, joyriding, public nuisance."

"Nice. Still doesn't explain why she's phoning here, though," Quinn muttered. "Moss, you're local plod. Ever arrested her?"

"Once or twice," Moss said. "When I was in uniform."

"She's a good kid," DC Patel added, "though she sometimes falls in with the wrong crowd."

Quinn pulled a face. "Yeah, yeah, my heart bleeds. Why is it parents always say their kid's a saint, even when they're out mugging grannies? She'll be on *Britain's Most Wanted* in a couple of years, you mark my words."

"Mr Quinn!" Heidi said. "I've already told you I know her mother and she's doing her best. I'm sure Donna isn't a bad kid."

"Are you saying that because you believe it, or because she's your son's girlfriend?"

"Arun doesn't have a girlfriend!"

"Fine," Quinn said. "Let's call the school. Find out if our young Mother Teresa is in class today. If she's not, then we find her and bring her in."

29

10:55

"What's with all the chat downstairs?" Donna asked Arun when he returned to the study.

"I don't know. I didn't stop to listen. I think they're getting stressed. That's what usually happens when you put a lot of adults in a room. The alpha males are probably jockeying for dominance or something, like on David Attenborough."

"What did you go for?" Sam asked.

"This." Arun slipped a cylindrical object, wrapped in a handkerchief, from his blazer pocket. He laid it on the carpet and uncovered it to reveal a drinking glass.

"It's from my dad's bedside cabinet. He keeps it there so he doesn't have to get up at night if he's thirsty." Arun held the glass up by its base and squinted to see if there were any marks on it.

"Breathe on it, or hold it against the light," Donna suggested.

Arun brought his mouth close and breathed warm air on the glass, misting it. He quickly examined the surface before the condensation evaporated. A clear thumbprint showed on one side and three fingerprints on the other.

"Sam, there's a laser printer behind you," he said. "Can you get me the waste toner cartridge?"

Sam found the printer on one of the bookshelves, opened the front cover and located the plastic box in the lower right corner.

"Here you go," he said, sliding it out. He handed Arun the container.

Arun laid a sheet of white paper on the desktop and gently tipped a small amount of black toner powder on to it. He then rolled the paper up to form a tube and carefully lifted the tube over the side of the glass, tapping gently so that a fine stream of powder cascaded down and bounced off the shiny surface.

When he was done, he blew softly on the glass to dislodge any loose powder and held the glass up. There, on the side, were the three fingerprints, as clear and as black as if they had been inked on to the glass.

Donna handed Arun a roll of sticky tape from the desk tidy and he bit off a short length.

"Use the top one," Sam said. "Usually, it's the right index finger these things scan for."

Arun's tongue poked out of the side of his mouth as he concentrated on lining up the tape with the fingerprint on the glass.

"You've only got one shot," Sam warned. "Smudge this and we're stuffed."

Donna held the glass steady as Arun brought the tape to rest lightly on the print, before lifting it off.

"*Ta-daa!* Nice one," Donna said, as Arun held the print up to the light.

He tore off a second piece of tape and pressed its sticky side against the black lines and whorls to seal them in. "There. That should hold it," he said. "Now, where's that scanner?"

"I should warn you, this probably won't work," Sam said.

Arun and Donna looked at each other and shrugged.

"We can't give up that easily…" Arun muttered and slid the sticky tape over the scanner.

It bleeped softly and a message appeared on the flat screen: *Fingerprint not recognised. Access denied.*

"Try again," Sam said. "This time put your fingertip behind it, in case it's looking for skin tone or pressure."

"OK." Arun wound the sticky tape round his finger and slid it over the scanner once more.

The computer beeped again and repeated the message: *Fingerprint not recognised. Access denied.*

"Should've known it wouldn't be easy as this," Sam said.

"Stupid thing."

Donna was staring at the glass, which was still in her hand, when a thought occurred to her. "Let me see that print," she said to Arun.

He gave her the strip of tape and she held it up. She then took the glass and retraced what Arun had done with the tape.

"I know what you did wrong," she said, smiling.

"What?" Arun asked.

"It's back to front. Look. You pressed the tape like this, see?" She mimed the act of touching the tape against the glass. "And then you peeled it off, put it down and stuck another piece of tape on top of the sticky side. So, when you picked it up, it was already upside down. You're showing the scanner a reverse print. Here."

She turned the tape over, placed it against her finger and slid it over the sensor again.

There was a bleep and the on-screen message read: *Fingerprint accepted. Login initiated.*

"We're in!" Sam said, punching the air.

"Not so fast," Arun said. "Look."

The display now showed: *Enter username and password.*

"This is ridiculous," Sam said. "I just hope whatever's on this flipping laptop is worth all the effort."

"My dad's in trouble," Arun said. "If there's anything on this computer, anything at all that can help him, then we have to try."

Bored, DI Moss wandered into the open-plan kitchen and dining room at the back of the house.

A photograph sat in a frame on the sideboard, half hidden by a forest of *Happy Anniversary* cards. He picked it up and saw a twelve-year-old boy wearing a blue school blazer smiling back at him. Even though the boy's mouth showed a shy lopsided smile, the brown eyes remained guarded and serious, looking up from a floppy mop of chestnut hair.

Moss put the picture back and was startled by the staccato cackle of a magpie from the garden, louder than he would have expected from indoors. He went to the back door and saw it was slightly ajar, as if someone had pulled it in but not fully closed it. A patch of dark mud smeared the mat. Moss crouched, touched it and noted it was damp.

"Hey, gaffer, you were right," Green said from the living room. "Donna Critchlow didn't turn up for school this morning. A teacher swore he'd seen her before class but she didn't register."

"That's strange," Quinn said. "What kind of truant goes to school first and then bunks off?"

"That's not all," Green added. "One Arun Lal also missed class today. Last seen in the corridor getting a cuddle from Donna."

Quinn grinned at Heidi. "Told you."

Heidi's mouth curled into a sneer. "If they've both run off together, as you seem to delight in thinking, then why would she phone here? Surely she could just whisper sweet nothings into my son's ear?"

Quinn's smile vanished. "Good point, well made. So where is she?"

"And where's my son? He isn't the sort to skip school. It's completely out of character."

"You think he's gone missing too? Hadn't thought of that. Brown, you checked upstairs?"

"Yes, boss."

"Go and check again. Properly."

Brown made for the stairs.

"But before you do," Quinn added, "get us another round of teas. And see if you can find some biscuits too. I'm starving."

11:13

"Your dad built this himself?" Sam asked, as the three children crowded round the laptop.

"Yeah, he's like a genius with computers," Arun said.

"Hmm... A password for this level of security usually asks for eight or more characters, with upper and lower case, plus numerals," Sam said.

"Can't we run one of those phishing programs that hits it with thousands of passwords until it gets the right one?" Arun asked.

"I don't think so..." Sam said. "Normally you get three attempts and then it throws you out."

"So we have three shots to suss out your dad's password?" Donna said. "Talk about Mission Impossible."

"Maybe not," Sam said. "Most people tend to use the same passwords for multiple accounts. It has to be something you can remember easily; there's no point creating the world's best password if you forget it. Names of pets or loved ones are popular, and your dad isn't expecting anyone else to log in."

"What's the most common password?" Arun asked.

"*12345678*, if you can believe that, followed by *password*."

"Too obvious. OK ... let's try this..." Arun muttered, his fingers hovering over the keyboard.

Under *Username* he typed, *Lal_kr*.

"How do you know that's his username?" Sam asked.

"I saw him key it in once before."

"Pity you didn't remember his password."

Arun bit his lip and typed in *Heidi1977*.

"The year Mum was born," he said, and pressed enter.

Password incorrect. Access denied. You have two more attempts appeared on screen.

"Great," Arun said. "Any ideas?"

"Did your dad have a favourite pet when he was growing up?" Sam asked. "How about his mother's maiden name? Place where your parents first met? What's the most important thing to him?"

"OK, OK. That's really not helping, you know. Too many options."

Arun took a deep breath and typed in *Arunjeet12*.

"What do you think?" he asked, his finger hovering over the return key.

Sam shrugged. "I dunno. It's as good as anything."

"Nah," said Donna. "Doesn't feel right to me. His son's

37

name and age? Too wussy."

"What would you know about it?" Sam blurted. "Not all dads are criminals."

"You—" Donna raised a fist and was about to lunge for Sam when Arun's finger jabbed the enter key.

Everyone stopped to look at the computer screen, which read: *Password incorrect. Access denied. You have one more attempt.*

"That's it then," Arun said with a sigh. "I was so sure there was something in here that could help. Stupid, really." He sat back. "I suppose we should leave this to the professionals. We're never going to guess this."

"What now?" Sam asked. "Go back to school? Wait to be caught for truancy? My mum's going to kill me."

"I told you that password was no good," Donna said.

Arun slid the laptop over to where she was kneeling.

"All right," he said. "You have a go. Maybe you're better at this stuff than we are. Use your female intuition."

"Are you mad?" Sam gaped. "How is *she* going to—"

"Shhh. Let her think."

Sam stared at Arun as if he had just sprouted another head.

"Take your time," Arun said. "There's no rush."

"Right," Donna said. "I need to think like a bloke... Let me see ... what's the most important thing to a bloke...?" She looked around again, eyeing the certificates and diplomas on the wall.

Sam folded his arms and leaned back. Arun chewed his lip.

"How about...?" Donna leaned over the laptop and typed: *Shearer09*.

"What's that supposed to mean?" Sam asked.

Arun facepalmed and nodded towards the signed football shirt.

Donna hit the return key. "I can't look," she said, closing her eyes.

Sam groaned. "Access denied. We're locked out. I knew it."

Donna's face fell and she opened her eyes, looking for the lock-out message.

"Where's the message gone?" she said.

Arun grinned. "You, Donna, are a genius. We're in."

"But, I thought—"

"I think Sam was getting his own back on you." Arun smiled. "There's no lock-out message because we're not locked out."

Sam moved out of Donna's thumping range.

"How did you know?" Arun asked her.

Donna pointed to the wall. "The Newcastle shirt. What else could it be? He's the only good player they've ever had."

Arun took the laptop from her and started tapping keys as Donna and Sam leaned over. "Right," he said. "Let's find out what's so important that it's worth kidnapping my dad for."

Down in the living room, Brown finished his tea and moved purposefully towards the stairs.

11:29

"What are you looking for?" Donna whispered.

"I don't know," Arun replied, tapping away at the keyboard. "I'm hoping we'll know when we see it."

"Try Recent Documents," Sam suggested. "See what was last being worked on."

"Good idea..." Arun said, sliding his finger over the touchpad. "There's a PowerPoint presentation in here. I wonder if that's what Galahad was after."

He opened the program, clicked on the File menu and slid the cursor down to the list of recent files. He stopped. "What's this? *Project MANDROID System Overview*?"

"That sounds interesting," Sam said, with one eyebrow raised. "Open it up."

A large slide appeared on the screen, with a column of smaller slides on the left. As Arun quickly scrolled down, his eyes widened and he whispered, "Oh. My. Gosh."

"What is it?" Donna asked, glancing over his shoulder.

Arun skimmed through the slide set calling out headings. "There's all kinds of stuff in here ... artificial intelligence, quantum computing, neural networks, stealth capabilities, cloaking fields, polymorphic meta-alloys, fusion-power cells, scramjets, silicon photonic chipsets, pulse detonation engines, nanotechnology... This is insane."

"Doesn't sound much like banking to me," Donna said.

"Arun..." Sam hesitated. "That's some pretty hardcore cutting-edge technology there. Does your dad write science fiction?"

Arun shook his head. "Uh-uh. There's photos and design specs in here. Looks like they're building something."

"What, your dad and this Galahad geezer?"

"Yeah ... looks like a fleet of vehicles."

"Someone's coming!" Sam said.

Arun snapped the cover of the laptop shut and dived for the door. He opened it a crack, saw Brown's shadow appearing on the stairs and estimated he was no more than halfway up. Arun tiptoed into his parents' room, quickly followed by Donna and Sam, and softly closed the door just as Brown appeared on the upstairs landing.

The three children leaned against the door, their hearts hammering against their ribs.

Brown reached for the handle of the bathroom door to his

left, went inside and undid his zip.

Donna wrinkled her nose as she heard the gurgle of a stream of liquid.

"It's all that tea they've been drinking," she whispered.

"How do we get out?" Sam mouthed, his eyes darting around the room.

"Follow me," Arun said. "You remember when the fire brigade came to school and kept banging on about planning your escape route? I listened." He went for the window, unlatched it and pushed it open.

Sam looked out and saw the tiled roof of the kitchen extension sloping away towards the back garden.

"We can't go out that way. They'll hear our feet on the roof."

"I've already thought of that," Arun said. "Now come on."

Brown had been brought up well; he wiped the rim of the toilet bowl, pressed the flush, washed his hands, dried them on a Batman towel and went back to the landing.

It was then that he noticed the study door was ajar. He knew he had closed it earlier, which meant—

Brown rushed to the door, Glock 37 in hand, and kicked it open, levelling the pistol to cover the room.

He assessed the situation immediately: the swivel chair had moved; a desk drawer was open; waste toner and stationery items were scattered around.

Brown kneeled to touch the flattened carpet in front of the desk. Still warm. He sprang to his feet and dashed into the master bedroom.

The room looked the same as he remembered it, except something was not quite right. He scanned the room, trying to compare it with the picture in his mind. And then it clicked: the scatter cushions were missing.

He went over to the bed, eyes searching the carpet, listening. He ducked down to look under the frame. The dust had been disturbed. Someone had been hiding under the bed, but when and for how long?

He went to the unlatched window, looked out and saw the four missing cushions in a line on the roof. It was going to be fun explaining this to his boss...

Downstairs, DI Moss had wandered back into the kitchen while DC Patel waited in the car out front. In the living room the secret service agents were squabbling over the remaining crumbs in the biscuit tin, as Heidi struggled to retain control.

A dull bump sounded from overhead. Moss looked up

and listened. There were more muffled thuds, like someone kicking a stuffed toy.

He went to the back window and looked out into the garden, expecting to see an overfed cat jumping from the roof.

Instead, he saw a trousered pair of boy's legs dangle over the roof edge, get a foothold on the back of the garden bench beside the house and jump down. Moss recognised the tall skinny boy immediately as Arun Lal.

As he watched, Moss couldn't stop a wide smile from spreading across his face. Donna Critchlow appeared next and then both she and Arun helped a chubby blond boy down. The three children disappeared round the side of the house.

Moss slipped out after them, speaking quietly into his police mobile.

11:43

"Will you stop doing that? You look like you're pregnant!" Donna laughed, pointing at the large bump under Arun's blazer as they walked among the crowds of shoppers on Richmond High Street.

"I want it where I can see it," Arun said.

The laptop was inside his school backpack and he had stuffed it under his jacket with both arms wrapped round it.

"Why do I feel like we're being followed?" Sam said, looking back.

"Because you're scared?" Donna said.

"Too right I'm scared. We have to get rid of that thing," he said, pointing at Arun's bump.

"No. Not if this is how we get Dad back," Arun replied. "We need to go somewhere we can get a better look at this."

Sam paused, a concerned look disturbing his freckles. "You know your dad's not a banker, don't you?"

Arun nodded. "I do now."

"Which means he's been lying to you all these years," Donna said, chewing her lip. "They're all the same."

"I'm sure he had his reasons," Arun said, looking away.

"Let's go to my house," Sam said. He checked his watch. "Mum'll be off soon for her afternoon shift, so we'll have a few hours with no one around."

Arun nodded, then brightened. "Do you still have that sixteen-terabyte external hard drive?"

"Yeah, but I haven't used it for a while. I got a two-terabyte memory stick for Christmas and it's a lot easier to carry."

"Good. We might need both."

11:46

Krishan Lal opened his eyes. Dazzling light blinded him momentarily and he squinted through his lashes, waiting for his eyes to adjust to the glare.

While they did, he noted his pounding head and bruised ribs. He might have a black eye from the airbag too. He was sitting on a metal chair, with his arms strained behind his back. He tried to move them but his wrists were bound. He flexed his fingers, noting a slight numbness and tingling at the tips: the onset of "pins and needles", meaning the restraints had been on for around fifteen minutes.

As his eyesight cleared, he saw that he was in a featureless white room with a table to the side. A webcam sat upon it, its spherical eye staring at him while the red light of a motion sensor blinked from the wall, and a row of powerful halogen lights bathed him in their antiseptic glow.

A soft click signalled a door opening behind him and he felt a rush of cold air, but no sound of accompanying footsteps.

"Professor Lal, how good of you to join us," purred a voice as rich and soft as double cream.

Krishan strained his neck but couldn't see the speaker.

"Here's where you're supposed to say: 'Who are you and what do you want from me?'" the voice said.

Krishan clenched his jaw and said nothing. The voice was a high flat monotone with no accent, revealing nothing about the speaker.

"If you *had* asked," the voice said, "you'd know I wouldn't answer the first question and you already know the answer to the second."

"There's been a mistake," Krishan said, remembering his training. "My name is Ravi Chandra. I'm a sales rep for a gaming company. Seriously. You've got the wrong guy. I'm not worth anything."

The sharp sound of one palm slapping another bounced off the walls. The applause ended abruptly. "Bravo, Professor Lal. And most impressive, I should add. I would have expected you to be confused, disorientated, malleable even, yet here you are, already trying to outwit your captors with that brilliant mind."

"You know I won't talk," Krishan said.

The voice laughed. "Ah, if I had a pound for every time

someone has said that to me, I could have retired years ago."

"Why don't you? I'm sure you've earned enough by now."

"Quite true, Professor, quite true. But you know why I do this: because I love my work. Nothing is more satisfying to me than breaking a man's will. The stronger the mind, the greater the challenge. How strong are you, Professor Lal?"

"Why don't you untie me and you can find out?" Krishan said, his lips twisting into a snarl. "Or are you only tough against someone who can't fight back?"

"Good. Very good. You seek to goad me, hoping I will succumb to emotion and make a mistake." The voice now came from a different place although Krishan had not heard any movement. "I like you, Professor. It will be such a shame to break you. Let me offer you a deal: tell me the combination to the safe in your office and I assure you a quick and painless death."

Krishan laughed. "Now who's playing games? If I give you the combination, I'm no longer of value. Until then, you need me alive."

"As you wish, Professor. As you wish. Allow me to fetch my little toys, and then we can play some more. Don't go away. I'll be back in two shakes of a lamb's tail."

The door closed and all Krishan could hear was his heart pounding and the quiet ticking of his watch.

12:02

Arun, Sam and Donna lingered round the corner from 4 Whittle Avenue, stalling until Sam's mum came out and set off for her afternoon shift at Tesco.

They hurried upstairs and into Sam's bedroom. At first sight it looked like a giant bag of rubbish had been emptied all over the floor.

Donna stared, open-mouthed, before she began to discern a semblance of order. Completely obscuring the carpet were mounds of circuit boards, heaps of computer magazines, piles of comic books, scattered papers, notebooks, empty drinks cans and crisp packets. Bookcases lined two walls, their shelves crammed with more computer parts and CDs.

"Oh my days," was all she could say. "Your mum lets you keep your room like this?"

With an embarrassed shrug, Sam cleared a path through the wreckage to a computer desk set up under the loft bed, and opened the curtains a crack.

Arun went straight to the desk, set the laptop down

and pulled open a desk drawer, removing a handful of flash drive memory sticks. "Where's the hard drive?" he asked Sam.

"Up here." Sam took a silver box down from a bookcase. It was the size and weight of a hardcover book.

As Arun pulled USB connector leads from the drawers and began plugging them in to the laptop, Donna ventured nearer the bookcases.

Arun flipped open the laptop and began logging back in.

"Hey!" Donna said, holding up a CD-ROM. "What's this?"

Sam and Arun exchanged a blank look.

"I dunno. Let me see it," Sam said.

"I know what it is," Donna continued. "You've written on it. It's *Star Wars*."

"So?"

"So? All morning I've had to put up with your snide jokes about me stealing things and here you are stealing films."

Sam wore the bewildered expression of someone who had asked for a Big Mac and received a salad instead.

"It's not stealing if you get it off the internet," he said.

"Of course it is! Listen, I've never stolen anything in my life, whatever you might think of me. Nothing. Ever. But that never stopped you getting up on your high horse and passing judgement on me, did it? You're a thief, a sneaky little thief!"

She marched to the bookcase, stumbling over a Pringles can, and started sifting through some of the stacked discs.

"*The Matrix* … *Terminator* … *Avatar* … *Doctor Who*… All nicked."

"You can borrow them if you like…" Sam squeaked.

Donna threw the handful of discs at him. "Don't speak to me!" she said, turning on her heel, glaring at the ceiling and counting to ten quietly, her fists clenched.

Arun, his face illuminated by the computer screen, looked at Sam and whispered, "She's right, you know. It is stealing."

Sam chewed his lip and blushed a deep beetroot colour. "I'm sorry," he mumbled.

"I said don't talk to me," Donna snapped.

"Yeah, but I am sorry – for all the mean things I said about you."

Donna ignored him.

"I believe you, though. That you never stole anything," he added.

"Guys," Arun said, "you need to see this. I mean it. *Now*."

His two classmates hurried to look over his shoulder. On the screen was a CAD drawing of a sleek fighter aircraft.

"Didn't we see that on the presentation?" Sam asked.

"Sort of." Arun toggled to the slide. "Except that here it's an actual photograph, not a mock-up. Whatever it is, it looks like they built it."

Sam leaned closer to look at the picture. "That's not like any aeroplane I've ever seen."

"There's more," Arun said, opening a new drawing. This time the spider-web outlines of a large multi-wheeled truck appeared. He toggled back to the slides and scrolled down to a photograph of the same truck.

No one spoke for the next five minutes as Arun opened up drawing after drawing displaying a variety of exotic vehicle designs, some with wheels, others with wings. In each case a corresponding photograph showed the finished version.

"I don't get it," Donna said at last. "Why is your dad's computer full of mad stuff like that? Is he a plane spotter?"

"These are detailed design drawings," Arun said. "Some of them go back years, judging by when they were saved. There's version control to track modifications, and there are tons of test reports, trial results, performance evaluations... The only person who would need all this stuff is the person building it..."

"Unless your dad nicked these files," Sam said. "Not that

he would," he added quickly, catching the look on Arun's face. "Let me check something..."

Arun slid aside and watched Sam open up Outlook and scan the email subject headings.

"Oh, no," Sam said. "You could be right... These are all dot-gov-dot-UK addresses ... and they keep calling your dad 'Professor'. Wow... There's so much cool stuff in here... From the headings I think your dad must be some kind of ... government scientist ... and this thing he's working on is code-named 'MANDROID'."

"Go back to the presentation," Arun said. "Show me the title slide."

Sam clicked through. The slide: *Classified: Top Secret. Project MANDROID System Overview and Outline of Current Capabilities. A Joint Presentation by Professor Krishan Lal and Doctor Galahad Thorne. 4 May.*

"'Current capabilities'?" Arun said. "You know what that means? They've built this thing, whatever it is, and it works. Dad was going to give a presentation about it today, but someone wanted to stop him. We have to figure out why."

12:07

As soon as the door clicked shut, Krishan Lal started working on a plan. He knew that at any moment the stranger could return with an array of tools to force him to talk. This could be anything from brutal instruments to subtler methods, such as a tub of cold water or chemical agents.

In either case it was better not to wait around and find out. Field agents were trained in resisting torture but Krishan had never volunteered for that kind of work. He much preferred the comfort of a nine-to-five job and coming home to his family every day, which was why, for all his brave words, he did not expect to hold out for long against any sustained torment. At the same time, if he was forced to talk and the wrong people took control of his work, then millions of people could die. By far the best idea was to avoid that situation, but how? His hands were tied behind his back and the chair was metal so unlikely to break easily.

Krishan closed his eyes, slowed his breathing and

focused his mind.

The key to solving a problem is to ask the right question, he reminded himself. Sometimes the only answer is to change the problem.

First things first. He would need to free his hands.

He let his mind explore the room, analysing it for anything that could be of use. It was about six metres long and four metres wide. The table stood a metre to his left and a bank of free-standing halogen lamps was about three metres in front of him. He could feel the heat from the high-intensity bulbs radiating on to his face. The webcam on the table was trained on him so his every move would be seen. He would have to disable the camera but, by doing so, he would alert anyone watching, so that would have to wait.

He flexed and twisted his wrists again, this time pulling and pushing as hard as he could. There was very little slack, which meant he wasn't wearing handcuffs. He interlocked both thumbs and pushed his palms outwards and down, to widen the gap between his wrists as much as possible. Sharp edges cut into his skin, telling him it wasn't rope binding him. He slipped his little finger into the gap and slid it up along his wrist towards his watch strap. It touched something hard and flat with a sharp plastic edge: a cable tie. Once he knew that, the rest was easy.

Krishan scraped and slid the chair across the floor until he was near enough to give the table a sharp kick upwards. Being lightweight with folding legs, it fell on its side, sending the webcam skittering. Krishan then bounced and shuffled his chair to the nearest halogen light. He slipped a foot under one of its tripod legs and lifted, overturning the lamp. It crashed to the ground, its glass face shattering but the bulb stayed alight.

Krishan positioned his chair beside the stricken lamp and leaned over. This part was going to hurt but he had no choice. The chair toppled sideways and he landed on his right shoulder, sprawling with his back to the lamp.

He thought he could hear distant shouts.

Thrusting his arms out behind him and using the warmth from the incandescent bulb as a guide, he brought his wrists nearer to the heat source.

There were definitely shouts now, and running feet.

The plastic cable binding Krishan's wrists melted the instant it touched the bulb and he sprang painfully to his feet. His arms ached and his legs were sore but he had no time to think about that.

The door opened and, as it did so, Krishan flung himself

at it with his full weight. There was a yelp as the door slammed into the head and arms of a man dressed in military fatigues, and an assault rifle fell from his hands. Grabbing the gun by the barrel, Krishan swung it like a cricket bat at the shins of a second man pushing his way into the room. There was a loud crack and the second soldier howled in pain as he fell.

Krishan yanked open the door and bolted into the corridor. Then stopped. On each side there were more soldiers, all levelling their weapons at him.

He dropped the gun and raised his hands.

12:15

"This is a nightmare!" Sam said, rubbing his hands over his face. "I just want to wake up."

"Shhh!" Arun said, opening yet another browser window on the laptop. "I think I've cracked this..."

Donna edged closer. "What is it then? And how much trouble are we in?"

Arun grinned at her. "Trouble doesn't even cover it. We've committed enough crimes already for them to lock us up for a thousand years."

"Good, so it don't matter if we add a few more."

"It matters to me," Sam said. "What'll my mum say?"

Arun pushed the laptop away. "Sam, I don't need this," he said. "I'll tell you what. You can walk away from this right now. Go downstairs, out of the door and walk down the road. Go back to school for all I care. But Donna and I are going to finish this. If that has to be without you, fine."

Sam wrung his hands and hopped from foot to foot as if he badly needed a wee.

"Sam, you're my best mate and I wouldn't get you in trouble," Arun continued. "I don't mind if you go, really I don't. I just need to know that if you're here to help, that you're going to stay focused and be useful. I can't take any more of your whining, all right?"

Sam nodded and blinked rapidly to hide the tears that were forming. "I'm in," he said quietly. "You're going to need my help."

Donna snorted but a look from Arun silenced her. "One thing we don't have is time," he said to both of them. "Let me tell you what I think this is about."

"I thought we were short on time," Donna said. "There's no need to show off how clever you are. I already know what this is about."

"Go on then," Arun said, raising an eyebrow. He folded his arms and leaned back in the chair.

"Your dad's a mad scientist. I should've guessed that from the start, knowing what you're like. He's gone and built some kind of crazy tool for the army and someone else wants it. Simple." Donna looked pleased with her theory.

Arun's jaw tightened. "Donna, my dad would never build a weapon, OK? I know him. He'd never do anything to hurt people."

"How do you know that? He's lied to you all these years about his job."

"That's different."

"How?"

"He probably just did that to protect me and Mum. What he's doing is obviously dangerous and he didn't want us to get hurt."

"Yeah, right. Look how well that's worked out. I'm telling you, man, he's built a weapon and someone else wants to nick it."

Arun looked to Sam. "Sam, are you going to hear me out? I know what this is and it's not a weapon."

Sam shrugged. "Does it matter what it is? It won't change anything. We're still in way over our heads."

"It matters to me," Arun said, placing the laptop on the floor where they could all see it. "Now, look at these pictures again." He toggled between photos of an aeroplane, a boat and a heavy truck, all coloured blue and gold. "The markings are consistent, so these are all part of the same fleet, right?"

Donna and Sam nodded.

"I went back through the email archive and found this," Arun said, flicking to an opened mail. He had highlighted the words: *MANDROID. Mobile Armour: National Defence/*

Rescue Operations – Initial Design.

"Mobile armour?" Sam said.

"For defence and rescue operations. It's specialised equipment for disaster relief."

"Is that it?" Donna asked. "So why all the fuss? Why would you kidnap someone for a ... for a ... bulldozer?"

"I have no idea," Arun said. "But if they want it that badly, I say we give it to them."

"Are you out of your freaking mind?" Donna said, grabbing Arun's arm. "After what they've done, you're just gonna give this to them?"

"If it gets my dad back, then yes. They want the laptop, so we give them the laptop – just not what's on it. That's why I've been copying the files."

"You know that if you just delete the files afterwards, that isn't going to stop anyone from recovering them?" Sam said. "If these guys are any good, they'll just put it all back together again."

Arun pursed his lips. "What else can we do?"

"You could rip out the hard drive and scrub the disk with an angle grinder, although that's a bit crude. Or you could use a good file-erase program like BCWipe. Use that and nothing's ever coming back."

"Do you have it?"

Sam edged away from Donna, who was picking her way through his collection of copied games. She stopped to pick up a *Doctor Who* Dalek voice-changer toy.

"Yeah, but it's a pirate copy," he whispered.

Arun sighed. "Donna, we're going to need to use some of Sam's illegal software to wipe this laptop clean. Will you let us do that?"

Donna stopped to consider this. "Two wrongs don't make a right ... but I like the idea of using one set of stolen goods to destroy another. There's a kind of justice in that... OK, do it."

Sam dived into a stack of CD-ROMs, searching for the program.

"And, Arun..." Donna said, keeping her voice low, "thanks for asking."

12:26

Krishan Lal was back in the white room.

He had been returned to the chair, only this time a whole roll of duct tape went round his knees, waist and chest, securing him firmly. There was so much tape round him that Krishan thought he must resemble an Egyptian mummy.

When the soldiers had finished binding him, they filed out, leaving Krishan alone again in the white silence.

He struggled to move, but only his head and neck were free.

The door clicked open but there was no other sound.

"Professor Lal." It was the strange high voice again. "I leave you alone for a few minutes and look at the mischief you cause."

Krishan said nothing.

"I need the combination to the safe in your office and I need it now."

A wheeled trolley slid into view and Krishan's heart skipped when he saw a white towel with a wicked array of stainless-steel surgical instruments laid out upon it, all glittering in the bright lights. The sight made him dizzy.

"Now, Professor Lal, are you going to tell me the combination or are things going to become ... unpleasant?"

"I can't tell you. If I do, then I have no value and you'll kill me."

"Krishan, Krishan, Krishan. There are worse things than death."

A white-gloved hand reached down to the lower shelf of the trolley and selected a hypodermic syringe and a small glass vial.

"Sodium thiopental," the voice said. "Some people call it 'truth serum' but it doesn't work that way."

The figure moved behind Krishan.

"Rather than force you to tell the truth, it just makes it harder for you to lie."

The figure grabbed Krishan's hair and pulled his head to one side, exposing his throat. Its other hand jabbed the needle into a vein and pushed the plunger down, emptying the chamber, before removing the needle and pressing down on the wound with a square of gauze.

"It takes a few minutes to work. Then you'll feel nice and warm and relaxed and we can talk about MANDROID."

"How do you know about that?"

"It's worth a lot of money to the right people. An undetectable weapons-delivery system capable of penetrating any country's defences. Just imagine, you could plant an atomic bomb in the heart of Paris, Tel Aviv or New York, then sneak away and no one would ever know – until it was too late, that is."

"It's not a weapons platform! It's designed for search and rescue. To help dig survivors out of fallen buildings—"

The unseen figure laughed: a high-pitched giggle with the quality of nails scraping a blackboard. Krishan imagined whoever it was wiping away tears of mirth.

"Is that what they told you?" the voice said. "Ah, of course... Someone as idealistic as you would never agree to build a weapon, so they had to lie to you, make you believe it was to help people. Dear, oh dear. People are such fibbers, aren't they? And your own government too."

The figure walked into view. It was tall and skinny, wearing a lab coat and white gloves. A shock of orange hair sat upon its head like a bright cloud of candy floss. The figure stood with its back to Krishan, basking like a lizard in the heat from the halogen lamps.

"And to think, all this time you thought you were helping people, but you weren't. You were building a weapon instead. What a sick joke."

"No, it's not like that."

"No, it's not. It's not funny at all but you know what is funny? Me."

The figure spun round on one heel and Krishan screamed when he saw the skeletal face: ghostly white, with large staring eyes, jagged cheekbones, a blood-red nose and crimson lips.

"You've got to be kidding me," Krishan said. "I'm being tortured by ... a clown?"

12:30

Doctor Galahad Thorne stood by the picture window in his office, stroking his sculpted beard and talking intently on his phone. "No, Minister, no one's telling us anything... Yes, I do understand the implications..."

The view behind him was dominated by the dome of St Paul's Cathedral to the west and, to its right, the golden statue of Lady Justice atop the Old Bailey.

His personal assistant, Kevin Lewis, knocked and entered, waving his smartphone. "A call for you, sir, from—" he whispered.

"Minister, I'll call you back," Thorne said before ending the call. He snatched the phone from Lewis and listened. When he was done, he stared at the device.

"Something wrong?" Lewis asked.

"I don't know... Someone broke into Lal's house this morning and raided his study."

"What? But I thought MI6 was there."

"Precisely. Who would be so brazen as to enter a house full of secret service agents, steal something from under their noses, and get away again without being detected?"

Lewis frowned. "It takes some real nerve to do that. You think it's the Russians trying to muscle in?"

"Or the Americans," Thorne said. "Just because we're on the same side doesn't mean they wouldn't steal secrets from us. It's happened before."

"Did they take anything useful?" Lewis said.

"That's what I'm trying to find out. If someone else is muscling in, and they're this good, we have a new problem."

"They can't be after MANDROID as well?" Lewis asked, his voice hushed.

"Why not? It's cheaper to steal it than to pay for it. As we both know."

Thorne gazed out of the window. It was lunchtime and the streets were filled with office workers roaming in search of food.

"I don't like it," Thorne said. "If Mossad, or whoever it is, has sent a spy to steal MANDROID, we have a new, unknown quantity to factor in. It's bad enough losing the laptop because of a stupid wedding anniversary; the last thing we need is a foreign assassin on our tail. Tell Saipher to hurry it up."

"But you said—"

"Things have changed. Do whatever it takes. If we can keep Lal alive, fine. If not, I can live with that." Thorne smiled. "No pun intended."

Back in Sam's bedroom, Arun and Donna crowded round the laptop while his fingers danced over the keyboard.

"Hold on a minute," Sam said, looking up from the screen. "I just thought of something."

"Are you having second thoughts again?" Arun asked.

"No, it's not that. Look at this." He highlighted the Communications Suite icon.

"Yeah…?" Arun said, unsure of what Sam was getting at.

"There's a VPN, dedicated modem and encrypted Wi-Fi on this laptop. I've just checked the last transmission and there's a complete comms log."

"Which means what?" Donna said.

Sam fixed his eyes on Arun. "Remember that AI you were talking about earlier?"

"AI?" Donna repeated.

"Artificial intelligence," Sam said. "Machine learning. Arun, if this MANDROID thing really does have an AI, does that mean it could talk to us?"

Arun cocked his head to one side. "Maybe. It depends

how advanced it is."

"Given half the stuff in here, I'd say it's advanced enough."

"It would certainly help clear a few things up. Can you get the link working?"

Sam winked. "I just did."

"It is, of course, just a rubber mask," the clown figure said to Krishan. "Clever, no? If, somehow, you were to survive all this and the police questioned you, would anyone take you seriously if you said Pennywise the clown held you captive? Of course not."

"Why a clown?" Krishan said. "Why not Mickey Mouse, or Prince Harry?"

"Because you suffer from coulrophobia, a fear of clowns. You're already starting to sweat."

Krishan stared at the skinny figure. His mind felt as if someone had opened the top of his head and poured syrup inside. Thinking was a struggle; ideas floated out of reach like drifting bubbles. That would be the thiopental taking effect.

"How...? How would you know that?" he managed to ask, struggling to form the words.

"I've read your personnel files. I know everything about

you, Professor. All your strengths, all your weaknesses."

"But how would you...?" Krishan closed his eyes. "Ah, I get it... I see..."

"The combination to the safe, Professor. What is it? Tell me."

"It's Galahad, isn't it? This is his doing. He's behind this."

A musical ringtone went off.

Pennywise pulled out a mobile phone. "Yes?" The clown's large eyes were fixed on Krishan the whole time. "Oh, so you're finally listening to me... Yes, it won't take long... No, it'll be my pleasure... OK... By the way, he knows it's you. He just worked it out for himself... All right..." The call ended.

"Bad news, Professor. The time for a softly-softly approach is over. Now I get to do things –" the skinny figure went to the trolley – "my way."

The clown came back towards Krishan holding a scalpel. "You can scream if you like. There's no one in the world who can help you now."

12:33

"Is the speaker on?" Arun asked.

"Yes, and the mike," Sam answered. "I'm initiating comms ... now. Say something. It should be able to hear us, wherever it is."

"Uh, hello?" Arun said into the laptop. "Is anyone there?" He waited for a response, then shrugged. "This is silly."

"Try again," Sam urged.

Arun rolled his eyes. "Testing, one, two, three... This is Lal calling MANDROID. Do you read me, over?"

Good afternoon, Professor Lal.

Arun jumped at the sudden sound.

"It thinks you're your dad," Donna mouthed.

Have you been stricken with a cold or other physical impairment, Professor? The voice was soft, mild and gently modulated.

"No ... I'm fine." Arun's eyes flicked between Sam and Donna, imploring them for help. "Why ... do you ask?"

Your vocal range is higher than normal, hence I waited for you to identify yourself. A testosterone deficiency may cause a higher voice. When did you last have your testosterone measured?

"I don't have any hormone problems!" Arun snapped.

Oh. Perhaps your trousers are too tight then.

"Very funny. Can we change the subject?"

Certainly, Professor. How was your presentation received?

Arun covered the microphone and glanced up at Sam. "I can't believe I'm talking to a machine!"

"Like you've never heard of Siri?" Donna said.

Arun ignored her. "This is so cool! What do I say?"

"I don't know. Just keep talking," Sam said.

"Um, it went fine. They love me. And you. That'd be us. They reckon you're going to … going to… Remind me, what it is you're supposed to do?"

My primary function is to save lives, protect civilians and prevent harm to innocent people.

"See? I told you," Arun whispered to Donna.

My secondary function is now a weapons-delivery system.

Sam's jaw dropped while Donna smiled and chalked up an imaginary point.

"You what?"

It is as you suspected. Doctor Thorne has been making

unauthorised modifications, which were completed this morning.

"The sneaky rat," Arun said. "I knew it! What kind of unauthorised modifications?"

Doctor Thorne arranged for a non-standard item to be loaded into the cargo hold at eight-thirteen this morning.

"What do you mean by 'non-standard'? Is it a drinks machine?"

No.

"An Xbox?"

No.

"Then what?"

A B61 nuclear bomb.

Arun laughed out loud while Donna and Sam exchanged looks of alarm.

"Ha! Good one. You had me going there," Arun said into the laptop. "An AI with a sense of humour. So, come on. Tell me. What are you really carrying?"

A B61 nuclear bomb. It is a thermonuclear weapon with a two-stage radiation implosion—

"Stop!" Arun had his hands over his ears. "Just stop. Did you say you can function as a weapons-delivery system?"

Yes.

"And you're carrying an atomic bomb?"

Yes.

"Why?"

I do not know precisely. Would you like me to guess?

"Like, duh!"

Fact one: the MANDROID fleet is fully equipped with advanced stealth capabilities, making it undetectable. Fact two: it has recently been weaponised.

"So ... if it dropped a bomb on a city, no one would ever know who did it?"

Correct.

"But why would anyone want to do that?"

Conjecture: to prove it could be done.

"You mean like a demo? We have to stop this. Where are you?"

My location is classified.

"You can tell me."

Why would I tell you something you already know?

"Uh ... can I get back to you?"

Certainly, Professor.

Feeling queasy, Arun closed the laptop and looked at his two friends. "You heard all that, right?"

"Uh-huh," Donna said.

"Yeah," Sam squeaked.

"So it looks like we've got to stop Galahad before he

steals this MANDROID fleet and uses it to drop that bomb."

"Or we could call the police," Sam said.

Donna sucked her teeth. "Like they're gonna believe us? You can't trust the feds."

"No, we can't," Arun agreed. "If Galahad wants this laptop so badly, we give it to him, in exchange for my dad. Once we get him back, he can then override MANDROID and pull the plug on this whole thing. Let's go."

12:36

"Here it is," Arun said, handing Donna a note with a mobile number scribbled on it. "You know what to do?"

Donna nodded and keyed the digits into her phone. She switched on speaker mode, so they could all listen, and pressed her lips to Sam's Dalek voice-changer toy.

"Hello?" a man's voice said in a clipped accent.

"Doctor Galahad Thorne?" Donna said, her voice distorted into a harsh metallic rasp.

"Who is this?"

"You can call me Double-X."

A five-second silence. Then: "What do you want?"

"I have the MANDROID files you're looking for."

"You're bluffing."

"Check your email. I'll call you back."

Donna ended the call and mimed wiping sweat from her forehead. "How was that?" she asked.

Sam smiled and held two thumbs up, the signal for Arun to hit "send" on the email he had prepared.

* * *

Thorne stared at his phone as if it had changed into a scorpion, before scurrying round his desk to check his computer.

Sure enough, a brand-new email had arrived from Krishan Lal's account, with a large file attachment. Thorne clicked it open and sat down, clasping his hands to stop them shaking.

On screen was a design drawing for a sleek futuristic motorcycle.

The phone rang, making him jump.

"Did you get the mail?" rasped Donna's Dalek voice.

"Yes, I did."

"Do you still think I'm bluffing?"

"No, no. You have my full attention. What is it you want?"

"An exchange. Krishan Lal for the laptop with all the MANDROID data."

"What laptop?"

"Mr Lal kept a spare. It was in his study. Now it's with me."

Lewis knocked softly and came back into the office. Thorne looked up at him and silently mouthed the words, "Trace this call."

In Sam's bedroom the children waited for the long pause

to end and for Thorne to speak again.

"Don't hang on much longer," Sam whispered, checking the second hand on his watch. "In case they try to trace the call."

"I'm going to count to three and then hang up," Donna said. "One ... two..."

"OK. You have a deal," Thorne said. "Where and when?"

"Victoria station. At one-thirty. I'll call you then."

"That doesn't give me enough time. Make it two."

"OK. Victoria at two o'clock. Gotcha."

Sam brought one hand down against the other in a chopping motion, indicating for Donna to end the call.

She blanked him. "And, Thorne?" she said.

"Yes?"

"Don't try and get clever with me, or you will be *EX-TER-MIN-A-TED!*"

Donna hung up and then fell about in a fit of giggles. Sam gaped but Arun couldn't help laughing too.

Thorne slammed his fist down upon the desk.

"That's just what I was afraid of!" he said. "I told you this guy was good! Did you get the number?"

Lewis shook his head. "He wasn't on for long enough. What's he want?"

82

"Lal, in exchange for the MANDROID data."

"That doesn't make sense. He must know it's worth billions."

"Of course he does. That's why I don't like it." Thorne gnawed at a hangnail. "It's a trap. He has the same problem we do, which is he has the laptop but he needs Lal to open it."

"Is that why you asked for the extra half-hour?"

"Darned right it is. I'm surprised he agreed to it. Get some people down to Victoria right now. I want every exit covered. Stake the place out. And go armed."

"What about Lal?"

"We'll have to take him with us. If he isn't already dead."

12:39

"You have a wife, Heidi, and a son, Arun," the clown said, standing in front of Krishan and brandishing a scalpel in a gloved hand. "We did try to bring Arun here, you know, to help ... encourage you to cooperate."

"You didn't—"

"No, he ... declined the invitation. Nonetheless, should you survive this, I'm sure you would like to see him again."

Krishan's eyes were fixed on the scalpel.

"I will tell you what I'm going to do, Professor, so we are both in no doubt as to the choice you have: give me the combination to your office safe or I start removing parts of your body. Do you understand?"

Krishan nodded.

"I said, *do you understand*?"

"Yes," Krishan said, straining again at the straps and tape binding him to the chair, but it was no use.

Pennywise held up the scalpel, its blade glinting. "I am going to count to three... There will not be a four."

Krishan gritted his teeth and his top lip curled into a

sneer. "I can't tell you. There are too many lives at stake."

"That's fine. I gave you a choice. It's your decision, not mine. One ... two..."

"Don't do this... Please..."

The blade rested lightly on Krishan's ear.

"Thre—"

The phone rang.

The clown gave a shriek of frustration, threw the scalpel to the floor and grabbed the mobile phone.

"What?" the figure shouted, breathing in hard, rapid pants.

It stood stock-still, listened and then turned off the phone.

Krishan watched as the figure kneeled to pick up the scalpel.

"Professor," the clown said, turning back to him, "you are without doubt the luckiest man I have ever met."

Pennywise advanced, the blade glittering.

"You're going for a drive."

"Agent Double-X?" Arun said, munching on a Marmite sandwich in Sam's room.

"Yeah? So?" Donna said, popping a Hula Hoop into her mouth. "I had to think of something."

"It's a bit ... James Bond," Sam said. He was watching the laptop screen as it continued copying files to the external hard drive.

"It's chromosomes, innit?" Donna said, winking at him. "They'll never figure it out."

"And why Victoria?" Arun asked.

Donna shrugged. "It's the nearest big station. I mean, we haven't got a car, so it's that or the bus."

"Why Victoria?" Lewis asked, pacing the carpet in Thorne's office.

Thorne looked up from his computer and scowled. "What do you mean?"

"It doesn't make sense. Why do a hostage exchange in one of the busiest stations in London, with thousands of people at any given time? What's he playing at?"

"Think about it, idiot. Where better? It's central London. You have trains, buses, taxis and cars all around. There are multiple exits, shops, escalators, phone booths, you name it. Add in thousands of commuters on the move and you have the perfect place to hide in the crowd. I'm telling you, this guy is good."

"So how do we stop him?"

Thorne smiled. "Naturally, I have a plan."

Back at Arun's house, Green's phone rang. He answered it, listened and nodded.

"Gaffer," he said to Quinn, "it's the girl's phone. She made a call about ten minutes ago – to guess who?"

"Do I look like I'm in the mood for guessing games? Who? Lady Gaga?"

"Doctor Galahad Thorne."

Quinn ran a hand through his iron-grey hair. "The twerp who called here earlier?"

Green nodded.

"What are the odds of that? The only two calls we get here all day and now they're talking to each other... I don't like it. Why would a schoolgirl be calling him? Get a car round to the girl's house. Now! I want her found. You two, stay here and man the phones. I want the rest of you on the move. Let's go!"

The agents started to gather their gear. Quinn pulled on his overcoat and stopped as a thought occurred to him.

"And find out who else was off school today and cross-reference their names with Donna's class. Get me a list of addresses. Something tells me that if we can find the girl, we can get to the bottom of this. Move it! We can still put a stop to this before someone gets themselves killed."

13:08

Back in Sam's bedroom, he was stuffing the external drive into his Iron Man backpack. "We're lucky Thorne gave us an extra half-hour," he said. "We'd never have got those files copied otherwise."

"Did you get them all?" Arun asked.

"All the MANDROID ones, yeah. There was tons of other stuff but I don't know how useful it is."

Arun zipped the laptop into a black carrying case and adjusted the straps to fit.

"Did you wipe the memory?" Donna asked.

Sam nodded. "Yep. All the MANDROID data's gone. The rest of it still works, though. If I had more time, I could've cleared everything, operating system and all, but—"

"We need to get moving," Arun said. "We've been here too long. Sam, you got any clipboards buried in here?"

"Yes, why?" Sam said, digging through a mound of homework folders.

"If we're going to be standing around a train station in our school clothes, we'll need a cover story. The last thing we need is to get picked up for truancy."

Donna smiled. "You're learning fast."

"If we've got everything, let's go," Arun said, checking his watch.

Richmond station was a ten-minute walk from Whittle Avenue and Victoria station was another half an hour from there, thirteen stops on the District Line.

The children spilled out of Sam's house and hurried down the street, back towards the busy main road. In their haste none of them noticed a silver Audi pull out and drive slowly in the same direction.

As the three classmates walked along, Donna poked Sam and said, "How come your mum lets you keep your room like that?"

Sam shrugged. "Dunno. She just lets me get on with it. As long as I keep it out of her way, she doesn't care so much."

"Who buys you all that stuff? I mean, all that computer gear must cost a bomb and then there's the broadband."

Sam brightened. "That's my dad. He's cool."

"Why? Is he into all that?"

"No, he hasn't a clue. My dad's a builder, named Bob funnily enough. He runs his own business, but he's always said to me, 'Don't be thick like me, son. Learn how things work and get a good job, so's you won't have to stand in the rain and snow all day long, like I do.' He's very clever, knows all kinds of stuff, is dead good with numbers, but he doesn't have any papers to prove it. So it's important to him."

They reached Sheen Road and approached a small parade of shops.

"Quick!" Donna said. "In here now!" She grabbed an arm each and steered Arun and Sam into the nearest shop, a convenience store.

The turbaned owner glared at them from behind the counter. "Only two schoolkids at a time," he said, pointing to a handwritten notice on the door.

"What's wrong with—" Sam started to say, but Donna aimed a finger at the glass door.

Two black Range Rovers sped by. Donna waited for them to pass before stepping out of the shop. She watched the cars hurtle down the road and turn right into Whittle Avenue.

"Was that...?" Arun started to say.

Donna nodded. "Secret service dudes. Recognised the cars a mile off. Extra-long aerials. They're not exactly standard."

"Why would they be going to your house?" Arun said to Sam, who was slouching behind him.

"Maybe they saw us leave yours?" Sam asked.

"Nah, if they had, they'd have been after us a lot sooner," Donna said.

They each bought a can of cola and resumed the walk towards the station, this time keeping a watchful eye on the traffic.

"It's your phone," Sam said suddenly.

"Huh?" Arun and Donna said at the same time.

"Your phone," Sam said to Donna. "From when you used it at Arun's house. They traced it. And if they're tracking you, it wouldn't have taken them long to home in on me."

"But why look for us?" Donna said. "We haven't kidnapped anyone."

"No..." Arun said, "which means they don't know who the kidnapper is. They're clutching at straws."

"But wait," Sam said. "*We* know. Why don't we just tell them? Then we can let them clear everything up."

"They thought I was Arun's girlfriend," Donna said. "That's how dumb they are. If we bring them in now, they'll just get everyone killed."

They turned right on to the Quadrant, the busy shopping street that led directly to the station. Arun stopped by a bin and dumped the phone he had picked up earlier by the school gates.

"Anyway, I've told you about my dad," Sam said to Donna. "What about you? What's your dad like?"

"Getting kinda nosy, aren't you?" she said, looking away.

Sam reddened. "Me? Get lost! If you hadn't been so pushy, asking why police were at Arun's house, we wouldn't be in this mess in the first place. And you're calling me nosy!"

Donna exploded. "He's been banged up, all right? Is that what you wanted to hear? I know what the other kids say and it's true, all right? Happy now?"

The force of Donna's anger was like a gale, extinguishing everything in its path. They walked in silence for a moment before Sam's curiosity flickered back to life, like a trick candle that reignites after being blown out.

"What is he in jail for?" he asked.

Donna stopped and looked at Sam as if seeing him for the first time. She looked at his scuffed shoes, charcoal-grey trousers, up past the blue and gold school tie to his round pink face and sandy hair. His expression was one of genuine interest and there was nothing judgemental in his look.

She sighed. "Stealing, all right? My dad's a sneaky, grubby thief."

"Is that why—" Arun began.

"Yeah. That's why I've never done it, all right, and why I don't like people who do."

"What about your mum?" Sam asked. "What does she do?"

"She's a lawyer." Donna laughed. "She's the one who put Dad in jail. Tough as nails, my mum. Had a hard time growing up here. She came over when she was six and—"

"It's your mum who's black?" Sam blurted.

"Yeah, why wouldn't she—" The look of puzzlement on Donna's face faded like mist as realisation dawned. "Oh ... I get it. Dad gets done for stealing so you assume he's black and my poor single mum is white. I get it. Thanks. Thanks a lot." She turned on her heel to stomp off in the opposite direction. "Why don't you two both—"

"Shouldn't you lot be in school?" DI Moss said, stepping across to block her path.

13:22

As DI Moss's solid frame blotted out the sun, Donna looked up, shading her eyes.

"Can I help you?" she said.

Moss eyed the three children. "I said, shouldn't you all be in school?"

"Lunch break," Arun said, looking at his watch. "We're not due back until half one, so technically we're not skipping any classes."

Donna looked at him, her mouth open.

Sam waved a clipboard. "We're doing a shoppers' survey for a homework project. How often do you change your underpants?"

Donna smirked and stepped back to rejoin the boys. "Officer, are you going to arrest us, or just hassle us? Only make up your mind, cos we're in a hurry."

Moss raised his hands, palms outwards. "Look, I don't know how much you kids know about what's happening but I'm here to help."

"Aren't you the detective who—" Arun started to say.

Moss nodded. "Yes, and I know that you three were upstairs the whole time. Now ask yourselves why I haven't told anyone else about that little stunt."

Arun paused. "All right. Maybe you do want to help. Trouble is we have a train to catch and we don't have time to chat."

"Why don't we take the train together and you can explain on the way?" Moss started to walk towards the station. "Where are you going?"

"Ealing," Donna said, before Arun could answer. "We think Arun's dad's being kept there."

They reached the station and Arun checked his watch again. The train to Victoria would be pulling in to Platform Two any minute now.

"Why do you think that?" Moss asked.

"Uh, because of something that bloke from his work said," Donna replied.

Moss frowned. "I don't recall..."

Arun heard the clattering of the train approaching. His eyes darted around the ticket hall where a crowd of backpacked foreign students clustered round the ticket machines. The main concourse was clear but passengers would be charging up the stairs as soon as the train doors opened.

"Come on, guys," he said. "Let's get tickets."

Ignoring the quizzical looks from Donna and Sam, Arun crossed over to the ticket booth.

"What are you doing? We don't need tickets," Sam muttered as he joined Arun by the luggage gate.

"When I say move, you move. Do what I do. Understand?"

Sam swallowed hard and nodded.

"Tell Donna," Arun added, and busied himself collecting a handful of Tube maps and other leaflets from the dispenser next to the ticket window.

With a hiss, the train stopped and the doors opened.

The children edged nearer to the ticket gates. Beside the one on the end was a low square arch with rubber flaps hanging down for people to push suitcases through and, next to it, a bypass gate with a magnetic lock.

Moss looked up as the clattering of footsteps echoed up the stairwell from passengers hurrying off the train.

"Now!" Arun shouted, and flung the pamphlets into Moss's face.

In the split second of confusion that followed, Arun dived through the luggage gate, landing at the feet of the first startled commuters.

Sam jumped after him but was yanked backwards as the top of his backpack caught on the arch.

"I'm stuck!" he cried.

Arun grabbed his outstretched hand and Donna pressed down on the backpack and shoved as hard as she could.

"Hey! Watch what you're doing!" cried an angry passenger as the boys sprawled on the ground in front of him. Then Arun was on his feet, as nimbly as a cat, weaving through the commuters to get to the train platform. Bodies pressed against him: arms, chests, bags, coats. He heard the hiss of the doors, about to close.

Moss shoved a spotty teenager out of his way and lunged for Donna, grabbing hold of her arm.

She twisted and wriggled, slipping out of her blazer, and ducked through the luggage gate, leaving Moss holding the blue jacket.

As the train doors started to close, Arun grabbed hold of the left-hand door, and braced his foot against the bottom of the other to keep it open. The door pushed against his shoe but his weight held it.

"Come on!" he shouted over his shoulder. "Quick!"

Sam landed in a crumpled heap at the bottom of the stairs and scrambled though the gap. There was a hiss and a clunk as the train prepared to move. Donna appeared, moving with athletic grace and dived through the gap. Arun released the doors, which slammed shut, and there was a whirr as the train started to pull away.

The children watched through the window as Moss jumped down the last five steps to see the departing train. He ran alongside for a few metres, slamming his hand against the metal sides as it gathered speed and rumbled away.

The last thing he saw were three laughing faces squished up against the glass, tongues out and eyes crossed.

13:42

The boardroom door opened and two men entered, one wearing a navy-blue suit, the other a dark green British Army uniform.

"This way, please, General," said Clements, the younger man, leading the way to a table around which five men were seated.

"Ah, General McAllister, so glad you could join us at short notice," said a tired-looking man wearing frameless glasses. He stood and held out a hand. "I'm Project Director Brian Phelps."

McAllister shook hands, found a chair and sat stiffly.

"You should know everyone else here, by name if not by face," Phelps said, gesturing towards the four men seated round the table. "On your right is the Chair of the Joint Intelligence Committee, and the Minister for Defence Equipment and Support." The men nodded as their roles were stated. "On your left you have a representative of the Secretary of State for Defence, and an aide to the prime minister."

Phelps poured himself a glass of water from a jug in the middle of the table and took a sip. "Now that you're all here, we can begin," he said.

Clements switched off the lights. The momentary darkness was dispelled by a wall-sized plasma screen blinking into life.

"Gentlemen, what I am about to tell you is classified 'top secret' and cannot be disclosed to anyone outside this room without my express written permission," Phelps said, his body silhouetted by the blank white screen. "I needn't remind you that you're all bound by the Official Secrets Act."

Heads nodded in understanding.

"In 2002, as part of the British Government's response to the 9/11 attacks in America, the decision was made to create a new ultra-high-tech research and development directorate, dedicated to integrating cutting-edge technologies, with a view to protecting this country from future terrorist attacks. The code name for this initiative is CITADEL." Phelps spoke in a well-rehearsed manner.

"Does that stand for anything?" asked one of the suits.

"Coordinated Intelligence Taskforce: Advanced Defence-Engineering Logistics. CITADEL's remit is to think the unthinkable, to push the boundaries, to apply innovative solutions to age-old problems. To do this, we needed to recruit the finest minds."

A photograph of an elderly man smoking a pipe appeared on screen.

"We started with this man, Major Geoffrey Boothroyd. Some of you may know his work with the Secret Intelligence Service. We gave him free rein to decide the structure of this department and to select the personnel we needed."

The picture changed to show a much younger Krishan Lal holding a beer, with his other arm draped round the shoulders of a laughing Galahad Thorne.

"Among his first recruits were these two men, Professor Krishan Lal and Doctor Galahad Thorne. Krishan is, without doubt, a genius. It's an overused word, but in his case it's correct. Krishan has one of the finest minds of his generation and I can only thank God he's British."

"And the other one?" asked a minister.

"Galahad's good, very good, but he's not in the same league. Together, these two have been responsible for delivering Project MANDROID."

Murmurs of consternation rumbled around the room.

"Never heard of it," declared a listener.

"That's because disclosure of the MANDROID programme

is on a need-to-know basis only."

"And now we need to know?" the general said. "Why?"

"Because we have a problem," said Phelps. He took a gulp of water. "As of seven fifty-nine this morning, Professor Lal has gone missing."

"What do you mean by 'missing'?"

"I mean he left for work and failed to arrive. We've had no contact with him since Friday."

"Then you have a security breach," one of the government men said with a shrug.

"Perhaps, perhaps not. All our people were thoroughly vetted prior to joining the programme."

"Is it possible he could have done a runner? Defected?"

"No. Krishan is a family man, very stable. He wouldn't leave without his wife and son. The Secret Intelligence Service believes Krishan has been kidnapped."

"What?"

"But why?" asked another.

"Because Project MANDROID is ready to go live."

General McAllister fixed his steel-blue eyes on Phelps and said, "Just what is this MANDROID?"

Phelps glanced at Clements, standing by the door. "Please bring Galahad in. I think he's best placed to answer detailed questions."

Clements nodded and slipped away.

"Gentlemen, you may recall an incident in Myanmar in 2008," Phelps continued. "Cyclone Nargis struck that country, causing the loss of many thousands of lives. The international community rallied round to provide assistance but the military junta in charge refused their help, indirectly causing many more fatalities."

"I remember that," said the minister. "Disgraceful episode."

Phelps placed his palms on the table. "Now, imagine, if you will, a transportation system that is completely undetectable and capable of travelling at speed to trouble spots like Myanmar to help people on the ground. A system built for search and rescue in all environments, that doesn't need to wait on official requests for help because it can move without being seen. What would you say if I told you such a system exists?"

"I'd say you were crazy!"

"Completely untraceable?" said another. "Is that even possible?"

Phelps smiled. "MANDROID is that system."

"My god," said General McAllister, dabbing his forehead with a handkerchief.

The door opened and Clements poked his head inside.

"Graham, please show Galahad in," Phelps said.

"I can't," said Clements. "He's gone."

"Gone? Where?"

"I don't know. Lunch? He's not answering his phone."

One of the visitors leaned forward. "Are you telling us that both your lead scientists on this project have gone missing on the same day?"

Phelps nodded slowly, his mind churning.

"Director Phelps, just what the blazes is going on?"

13:48

The District Line train rattled through the tunnel towards Gloucester Road station.

Arun, Donna and Sam sat opposite an elderly lady who had a large handbag on her lap with a pug inside that was looking around. She glared disapprovingly at the children, but they ignored her, slurping their cans of cola.

Sam, sitting on the end, had taken the laptop out of its carrying case and put it on the seat beside him while he tinkered with some electronic equipment he had taken out of his backpack.

"What's he doing?" Donna whispered, watching Sam pop out a brand-new SIM card. She sat beside Arun. Her breath was warm on his ear and gave him goosebumps.

"Working on our plan B," he said, squirming.

"You know, what you did back there was pretty sick. Standing up to Moss like that."

Arun's head snapped round and he was suddenly eye to eye with his classmate. "Excuse me?" he said. "Did you just say I was ... cool?"

"There are no witnesses." Donna smiled, her white teeth flashing against plum-coloured lips. "Besides, I didn't say *you* were cool. I said what you *did* was cool."

"I thought you were going back to school." His voice was higher than he would have liked.

Donna laughed. "What, and leave you two to mess it all up? You need me if you're gonna do this, and you know it."

"But aren't you still mad at Sam?"

"I am, but what good's it gonna do? Besides, I'm used to it. It's hardly the first time."

"Yeah, I get it too. When my mum pushed me in the pram as a baby, some people asked if she was the nanny."

The train slowed as it pulled into Gloucester Road Tube station.

"Can I ask you a question?" Arun said, glancing up at Donna from under his floppy fringe.

"Yeah, go on then."

"Why are you helping me with all this? I mean, it's not like we're friends or anything."

"What else am I gonna do all day?" Donna stared out of the window. Her mouth tightened and twisted. Her brow knotted.

Arun waited.

"I dunno," she said, at last, her voice low. "Maybe ... it's just that … who knows…? If I'd maybe … loved my dad as much as you love yours, he'd still be around." She wiped her eyes with the heel of her palm.

Arun put an awkward arm round her shoulders. "Don't think like that," he said. "Whatever happened between your parents wasn't your fault."

Donna sniffed and shrugged away from Arun's arm. "Whatever."

"Three stops to Victoria," Sam said, a precision screwdriver behind his ear and a lithium battery in his hand. "Do we know what we're doing yet?" His eyes darted from Arun to Donna and back again.

"Maybe," Arun said. "Can you pull up that map of Victoria station again?"

Sam handed him his phone. "It's on here. Why?"

"I've got an idea."

The train slowed as Victoria came into view, and Arun, Donna and Sam darted out of the carriage.

"This is it," Arun said, checking the platform clock. "Victoria station in time for two o'clock. Let's go and rescue my dad."

In the CITADEL boardroom, Clements lowered his phone.

"Security says Dr Thorne left at ten past. His office was

locked and the blinds were down, so everyone assumed he was in there working," Clements said. "His assistant went with him."

Director Phelps was pacing.

"There's something else," Clements said. "Galahad's safe is empty and his network drives are missing. It looks like he isn't coming back."

Phelps punched the wall. "Darn it! Get on to the Intelligence Service. Tell them we have to find him. Fast!"

Clements dashed from the room.

General McAllister rose to his feet. "In case you haven't realised it, Director Phelps, a fleet of undetectable transport vehicles would make a formidable weapons-delivery platform. An enemy using it could strike without warning."

"Except the MANDROID isn't a weapon! I've already told you—"

"No, but it could be. What would it take to convert it, for example, to fire a missile?"

Phelps ran his hands through his hair. "Not much, General. I can see where you're going with this."

"And who has access to this fleet, beside your two scientists?"

"No one."

McAllister leaned closer. "So if one of them wanted to weaponise the system, who else would know?"

"I've already told you, that's impossible. Our people are completely loyal."

"I have a question," said the minister. "Where is this thing?"

"It's at a secret location. Only a handful of people know where it's kept."

"Does that 'handful' happen to include your man Thorne?" the general asked.

Phelps nodded. "Yes, but it's completely safe. It's guarded by a company of Royal Marines – and MANDROID can't be used without activation codes."

"Does Thorne have these codes?" asked another suit.

"No. Krishan keeps those on his computer."

"So as long as Thorne doesn't get his hands on Lal, we can contain this?"

"Yes."

"We'd better find him then. Before someone else does."

Galahad Thorne sat at a café table, looking out over the main Victoria concourse and sipping an espresso. Throngs of commuters bustled around, hauling shoulder bags, stooping under the weight of backpacks, walking wheeled suitcases and pushing trolleys.

His phone rang – a call from Lewis: "Sir, our people are in place. Lal's in a car outside, and we have teams covering every exit and someone on each platform."

"And the sniper?"

"Look up. The advertising hoarding to your right."

Thorne looked up to see a large poster advertising a Marvel movie that faced out over the concourse. The triangular slats revolved and the ad changed to one for Burger King.

"She's behind there?" Thorne said.

"Yes, sir. Full field of vision."

"OK then."

Thorne looked at his watch as a scruffy schoolboy wearing a blue blazer and an Iron Man backpack chugged past. It was 13:58.

"Just make sure everyone knows the drill," he said. "Under no circumstances is Lal to be allowed to leave with this Double-X character. Priority one is the laptop. Priority two is Lal. If we can take Double-X alive, that's a bonus. Otherwise, if anyone gets in the way, take them out. No mercy."

"All set?" Arun asked, checking his watch. His voice echoed

slightly inside the disabled toilet in which he and Donna were hiding.

Sam came in, gave them a thumbs up and stood guard by the door.

Donna nodded, picked up her mobile and put the voice changer to her mouth.

14:00

Thorne let his phone ring three times before he answered it. His hand trembled as he put it to his ear.

"Hello?" he said.

"Go to the passenger meeting point," the tinny Dalek voice commanded. "A payphone will ring in thirty seconds. Answer it."

"Hello? Hello?" There was silence from the phone. Thorne made a strangled noise, jumped up from his table and ran towards a pair of telephone kiosks by the meeting point. One of them started to ring.

"Out of my way!" he said, barging past travellers. "That's for me."

Thorne pulled a handkerchief from his trouser pocket, wrapped it round the telephone receiver and picked it up. He wiped the earpiece on his sleeve before answering. "Yes, yes. I'm here."

"Where is Lal?" the Dalek voice said.

"He's in a car outside. Where's the laptop?"

"It's with me. Take Lal where I can see him."

Thorne took out his mobile. "Bring him in," he said into it. He switched back to the payphone. "Where do you want him?"

There was a pause, and what sounded like whispering voices. "Bring him to where you are now. When I see him, I'll ring you back." The call ended.

Thorne's mobile rang. It was Lewis. "Yes?" Thorne said.

"Sir, what's going on? I thought we were calling the shots."

Thorne made a sour face. "This guy's a professional. He's probably got a rifle trained on me right now, and here I am, a sitting duck out in the open."

"It worked!" Sam said, his eye pressed against the crack of the toilet door, which he was holding slightly ajar. "There he is. Arun, I can see your dad!"

"Where? Let me see," Arun said, squeezing alongside Sam.

"Krishan! What an unpleasant surprise it is to see you again," Thorne said, as three plain-clothes soldiers marched Lal towards him.

He looked at Krishan the way a small boy might look at an insect before pulling its legs off.

"Galahad, you piece of— How could you?"

Thorne waggled a finger at him. "Uh-uh-uh. No questions. Not now. No time."

"Why? What's—"

The telephone in the kiosk rang.

"Someone wants you back, Lord knows why," Thorne said, and picked up. "All right, I've kept my end of the bargain," he said into the receiver. "Now it's your turn. Where's my laptop?"

"Say, 'Please'," said the metallic rasp.

Thorne nearly dropped the phone. "I'm sorry?"

"I said, 'Say, please.' Man, you are so rude, you know that?" said the harsh, vibrating voice. "Didn't your mother teach you any manners?"

Thorne looked around, bewildered.

"What's the matter?" asked Lewis.

"Please," Thorne said into the phone.

"Now say 'Pretty please'."

Thorne's shaking knuckles were white round the handset. "What?!"

"I said, 'Now say—'"

"All right, all right, I heard you! Pretty please. There, happy?"

A couple of tourists stopped to stare at the man in the

114

suit shouting at the telephone.

"What are you looking at? Get lost," said one of Galahad's men.

The couple ambled away, past a pair of armed police officers in high-visibility vests.

"Now say 'Pretty please with a cherry on top'," the Dalek voice said.

"Gah!" Thorne bashed the receiver against the coin box, his upper lip curling into a snarl. "Enough! Where do you want him?"

Sam was watching Thorne through the barely open door of the disabled toilet. His view was blocked momentarily by a pair of uniformed police officers armed with Heckler & Koch MP5 carbines.

Behind him, Arun squatted down to study a map of the station on Sam's iPhone while Donna was kneeling and speaking into her mobile through the voice changer.

From the other side of the wall a toilet flushed.

"Take him to the police station by the Hudson Place exit," Donna said, reading from where Arun's finger pointed on the map.

"To the police? Are you sure?" Thorne's voice said from the handset.

"You heard me. Once he's safe with the police, I'll tell you where the laptop is."

Donna ended the call and pressed the phone to her chest. Her hands were trembling and her heart was pounding.

"You're doing great," Sam said, and gave her a thumbs up.

"We're nearly there," Arun said.

Thorne put the receiver down and walked slowly back to Krishan and his men.

"What is it?" asked the man to Krishan's left.

Thorne looked at Krishan, the wheels in his mind turning. "Why hand you over to the police?" he said. "That makes no sense. Unless Double-X..."

He hurried over to a large map of the station. His finger jabbed the top-right corner marking the British Transport Police office and his eye was immediately drawn to the toilet block directly across from it.

"Of course... I thought I heard a flush..." He raised his phone. "Lewis, are you still watching Platform One?"

"Yes, sir."

"Double-X is positioned in the toilet opposite the police station. You're the nearest. Go and check. Flush him out if you have to, no pun intended. Get him to where the sniper can see him."

"You want me to go on my own to face this ... this...?"

"All right, you coward. I'll send one of the men with you."

Thorne beckoned the largest of the three soldiers and showed him the map.

"Hamish, see here? Go and check it out. Be prepared to shoot if you have to."

Hamish grinned, revealing a dazzling set of gold teeth.

"What about us?" asked the man holding Krishan. His diamond earring glittered.

"You two take Lal to the police station. Hand him over if necessary but don't let him out of your sight. This little game is coming to an end."

Sam, his eye glued to the crack in the door, waved his hand to get Arun's and Donna's attention.

"What is it?" Arun whispered.

"It's working! I can see your dad with two guys. Ooh, they look kind of big." He continued to watch for a few seconds, then pulled the door shut and locked it, eyes wide.

"What's the matter?" Donna said.

"There's two more of them, and they're coming this way. We're trapped!"

14:07

The tyres of the silver Audi Q5 screeched, smearing black streaks on the tarmac. The car skidded to a stop by the double yellow lines on Terminus Place, outside the main entrance to Victoria station.

DC Patel unclipped her seat belt and grabbed her bag, pulling her phone out as she pushed open the car door. As her thumb was about to hit the dial button, the screen lit up to indicate an incoming call.

"Andy," she said, "I'm here. Outside. Where are you?"

DI Moss bounded up the escalator on the balls of his feet, taking the steps two at a time. He had called Patel the moment he had seen a bar of coverage appear on his phone.

"I'm just leaving the Underground station," he said. "I'm going to check in with the Transport Police – let them know we're here before we nose around."

"You're sure those kids are here?"

"No, but this is where the train terminated and it's the

118

biggest station to hide in."

"Let's hope you're right," Patel said.

Moss charged through the open bypass gate, flashing his warrant card, and ran out on to the station concourse.

The gold-toothed man accompanying Lewis stopped outside the disabled toilet.

Lewis, crouching in his shadow, whispered, "Someone's in there. I saw the door close as we came nearer."

"Good," Hamish said, his teeth glinting.

He eyed the door, looked around to make sure no one was watching, and then reached into his jacket, his huge hand closing round the butt of the Browning pistol in its shoulder holster.

Standing to the side of the toilet block and leaning against the brickwork for cover, he reached out with his other hand and rapped on the door, ready to jump aside in case bullets ripped through the wood.

"It's in use," came a high voice from inside.

"I need to take a dump. Now!"

"Can't you find another toilet?" the voice inside said.

"No, I'm busting. I'm going to count to three and then I'm going to break down the door, you hear me?"

* * *

119

Inside, Donna stuffed the voice changer into her backpack and Arun pocketed the iPhone.

"One," boomed the voice from the other side of the door.

"What are we going to do?" Sam hissed.

"Two."

"We've got no choice," Arun said. "Open it."

"Thr—"

"All right, all right!" There was a dull clunk as Sam unlatched the door.

Without warning, Donna launched herself against Arun, almost knocking him over. She flung both arms round his neck and pressed her lips to his in a fierce embrace. He gagged, his eyes bulging like a scalded frog's. Sam's jaw dropped.

Hamish yanked open the door and stopped, a sly smile spreading slowly across his face.

"Well, well, well," he said. "What do we have here?"

Arun managed to detach his lips from Donna's and stared at her, dazed. Sam, his face the colour of beetroot, looked up at the soldier.

The big man grinned. "Kids these days, eh? Shouldn't you be in school?"

Donna glared at him.

"And couldn't you find a more romantic place than this?" He turned away and grinned at Lewis.

"What was it?" Lewis asked.

"Nothing. Just some kids fooling around. Let's go and check the other toilets."

Sam sagged to the floor. Donna wiped her mouth on the sleeve of her blouse while Arun grabbed hold of the washbasin and spat into it.

"It wasn't that bad," Donna said while Arun rinsed out his mouth.

"That's easy for you to say," Arun said. "You kissed me."

"You kissed me back."

"No, I didn't."

"Yes, you did."

Arun decided against arguing further. "What did you do that for anyway?" he said.

"Did you have a better idea?"

"You could've kissed me," suggested Sam.

If looks could kill, Donna's glare would have splattered Sam over the walls and ceiling.

"Two things," Donna said, fixing her glare on both boys. "One: this never happened; no one ever speaks a word about this."

"Too right," Arun said.

"And two: it worked, so stop moaning about it."

Arun nodded, then broke into a grin. "Did you see his face, when he opened the door? That almost made it worth it."

Sam stepped out of the cubicle to peep through the window of the Transport Police office. He saw Arun's dad standing by the counter flanked by two men. Sam turned and gave Arun a thumbs-up signal.

"OK," Arun said. "Time to keep our side of the bargain. Remember to keep it short so they can't track it."

Donna dialled Thorne's number and reached for the voice changer once more.

Thorne picked up on the first ring.

"What took you so long?" he said. "We handed Lal over to the police five minutes ago, as you instructed. Now, where's my laptop?"

"Calm down, big man," said the metallic voice. "It's at the lost property office. Ask for a laptop that was just handed in. There's a luggage tag on it."

"Is there a name?"

"Yes. The name to give is Ivor P. Brain."

"Ivor ... P. ... Brain... Got it." Thorne thought he could hear sniggering in the background before the line went dead.

He spun round, looking up for a sign pointing to lost property, then phoned Lewis, who answered, "Yes, sir?"

"Did you find anything?"

"No. The toilets are clear. He must've seen us coming and got away."

"Darn... Meet me back here. I'm going to collect the laptop. Tell the others to keep an eye on Lal. We're not giving him up. He knows too much."

Sam turned from the window of the Transport Police office to make his way back to the toilet block – and walked straight into DI Moss.

The detective stuck out his leg and kicked the back of Sam's knee. The boy's leg buckled and he fell, sprawling, to the floor. Moss was instantly upon him, twisting Sam's arms behind his back and pinning him to the ground.

"Oww! That hurts!" Sam cried. "Child abuse!"

"Shut it!" Moss said, reaching for his phone. "This time you're not getting away."

14:15

Thorne entered the lost property office and strutted to the counter as if he owned the whole station.

The petite blonde woman working behind the counter smiled sweetly. "How may I help you, sir?" she asked.

"I believe someone handed in my laptop a short while ago," Thorne said.

"Can you describe it for me, please?"

"It's in a bag with a name tag on it."

The attendant went into a back room and Thorne heard her rummaging around.

"Can you confirm the name?" she called from the back office.

Thorne grimaced. "Yes, it's Brain. Ivor P. Brain."

The clerk came back with a smirk and a black carrying case. "Here it is, Mr P. Brain."

Thorne's hands leaped for it but the attendant slipped it beneath the counter.

"I need to see some identification, please," she said, still smiling.

Thorne slipped two fifty-pound notes across the countertop.

"I was never here, do you understand?" he said.

"Perfectly, sir," she said, and handed over the laptop in its case.

At the meeting point Lewis was pacing. He jumped when his phone rang.

"Yes, sir?" he said, seeing Thorne's name come up.

"Lewis, I've got the laptop. We're back on track. Prepare to move out. Tell the team."

"What about Lal?"

"Give it a few more minutes. Double-X will have to make his move. If not, we'll just take Krishan with us and dispose of him later."

"You still think this Double-X character will show up?"

"Oh, yes. I hardly think he'd go to all this trouble to set up an exchange and then not collect his half. Just sit tight. And remember, I want him alive if possible."

"I don't believe it. What's *he* doing here?" Donna said, looking out through the crack of the toilet door to see Moss pinning down Sam.

"It doesn't matter. We have to help Sam," Arun said,

placing a hand on the door.

"What, and get ourselves nicked? Then how are we going to help anyone, let alone your dad?"

Arun hesitated, uneasy at the thought of abandoning his friend. "So what do we do? Leave him?"

"For now, yes."

"Get off, you're hurting me!" Sam cried, as Moss planted his knee firmly on the boy's back while juggling his phone.

"Quiet, I'm making a call," Moss said. "Sunny?"

"Where are you?" Patel asked.

"On the concourse, in front of the Transport Police office. I've got one of the brats here and I need to find the others. Can you come and pick him up?"

"On my way."

Moss ended the call and stood up. Sam scrambled to his knees.

"What did you do that for?" Sam asked, rubbing his back.

"What kind of a stupid question is that?" Moss said.

"We haven't done anything wrong. You can't arrest us."

"Listen. I don't know what kind of silly game you children think you're playing but this is serious business. A man's gone missing and you're—"

"I know. We found him for you."

Moss froze. "You what?"

"I said we found him. That's what we've been doing. Rescuing Arun's dad, no thanks to you."

"What? Where is he?"

"Right behind you. That's what I've been trying to say."

Moss spun on his heel and looked through the police station window.

"Stay here, you – and don't move!" he said to Sam, before running for the door.

Thorne strode over to Lewis, the laptop case in hand.

"All done," he said. He grinned and patted it. "I have my codes. We're back in the game."

Before Lewis could reply, his phone rang. He picked it up, listened and the colour drained from his cheeks.

"Sir, you were right," he said. "Double-X has made his move."

14:22

Krishan Lal stood behind a pink-haired Japanese student wearing a Hello Kitty backpack.

The officer standing behind the counter in the small police station was taking notes on a pad.

"Where did you last see your bag?" he asked, carefully enunciating each word.

"*Chotto matte, ne?*" the girl said, flipping through a phrase book.

The policeman lightly drummed his fingertips on the desk.

"Uh, Officer," Krishan said.

"Could you wait your turn, please, sir?"

"It's quite import—"

"We don't mind waiting now, do we?" said the soldier with the diamond earring on Krishan's right. The other trooper, wearing a black beanie, stood to his left. "We have plenty of time."

"Here," the girl said. She pointed to a word in her dictionary.

"Pharmacy?" the policeman read. "Ah, I see. *Boots* or *Superdrug?*"

"Yes, yes," the girl said.

The door crashed open and DI Moss burst into the small office.

"Krishan Lal!" he said, pointing.

There was a moment of stunned silence, before Krishan slammed his elbow up into Earring Man's nose. Cartilage crunched and, as he fell backwards clutching his face, Beanie reached for his Browning, a move that Moss instantly recognised.

The detective charged the bigger man, thrusting his right elbow upwards to prevent him from drawing the gun. Thrown off balance, Beanie stumbled and crashed against the counter. Moss clung on, keeping both hands locked on to his wrist, stopping him from pulling out the firearm.

Krishan looked around, saw a red fire extinguisher beside the door and grabbed it.

Beanie spun, slamming Moss against the counter, and lashed out with a boot, catching him on the thigh. The detective fell and the serviceman drew the Browning, taking aim at Moss.

Beanie barely had time to look up before the fire

extinguisher hit him in the face with a dull clang. His finger jerked as his head shot backwards and – *BLAMM!* – the gun went off. The sound was deafening in the small room and the laminated glass of the front window turned into a sheet of cracked ice as the bullet punched through it, leaving a small hole.

Earring Man moaned and rose to his feet, one hand clutching his broken nose, the other raising his pistol, aiming groggily at Krishan.

Krishan took one look, shielded his face with his arms and dived through the window, landing on the concourse outside in a shower of shattered glass.

Sam jumped backwards and couldn't help blurting out, "Awesome!"

Earring Man tracked Krishan's movement with the gun and took aim.

"No!" Moss slammed into him before he could shoot, bowling him over.

"Kidnap in progress!" Moss yelled at the bewildered Transport Police officer. "Call for backup!" He dived for the fallen gun.

Outside, in the station, passengers and staff had stopped when they heard the gunshot, then stared as Krishan Lal crashed through the window. They didn't start running until the gold-toothed soldier approached from the toilets, drew his pistol and levelled it at Krishan, who was getting to his feet.

"And where do you think you're going?" Hamish said.

"Police! Freeze!" Moss said, taking aim at Hamish from the doorway.

"Police! Freeze!" shouted a voice from behind Hamish.

"Are you kidding me?" Hamish said.

He raised his hands in the air and craned his neck round to see two armed police officers approaching with Heckler & Koch carbines at the ready.

"You, in the doorway, with the gun, hands in the air now!" said the police marksman.

"I'm a police officer!" Moss said. "This man is a criminal."

"That's what they all say. Put the gun down. Now!"

Moss swore and placed the gun on the ground.

Sam backed away towards the disabled toilet, as two more armed police officers approached from the main station, sub-machine guns in hand.

"What's going on?" one of them shouted.

"Don't know yet," the first one answered. "Maybe a robber— *AAAAGHH!*" He fell, clutching his knee.

Krishan saw something ricochet off the man's leg and

rebound off the polished floor.

Hamish smiled as the other three officers dropped in succession, each rolling on the ground, screaming and clasping their legs. He kicked their guns out of reach.

All around was pandemonium: people running for the exits, screaming, pushing and trampling each other. Sam ran straight for the toilet and hammered on the door.

"Let me in, let me in! It's me— *Urk!*" The door opened and two pairs of arms yanked him in so hard that he fell, landing on Arun and Donna.

"Oww! Geddoffme!" Donna yelled and kicked herself clear.

"What's going on out there?" Arun said, pushing Sam off his leg. "It sounds like a zombie apocalypse!"

Amid the chaos of panicked travellers rushing for the exits, several men moved calmly in the opposite direction towards the eye of the storm.

"Who's your friend?" one of them asked, his pistol aimed at Moss as he approached.

"This is the famous Double-X," Hamish said with a smile. He walked over to Moss, and picked up the relinquished gun. With a pistol in each hand, he motioned for Moss and Krishan to start moving.

"Remember, there's a sniper up there with a gun trained on you at all times, so don't try anything stupid. They might only be rubber bullets but, as you can see –" he kicked one of the police officers writhing on the ground – "she's a good shot and they do the job." Hamish cocked his head towards the Transport Police office. "Go and get the other two," he said to one of the newcomers. "We'll meet you outside."

DC Patel had reached a kiosk selling watches when she heard the first gunshot. She broke into a run, heading towards the sound – and ran straight into a tsunami of wild-eyed commuters stampeding towards the exit behind her. Lowering her head, she led with her shoulder and pushed her way through, ignoring the buffeting and bruising.

As the crowd thinned, Patel caught a flash of blue blazer disappearing into a disabled toilet. She raced towards it, then faltered, slowed and came to a stop as she watched four specialist firearms officers close in on a large man holding a pistol. In front of him, on all fours, was Krishan Lal and, to the right, in the police station doorway, DI Moss.

And then the four armed response officers fell to the ground one by one, clutching their legs. More armed men, wearing street clothes, converged from the train platforms. Patel's blood ran cold as she realised that she was in the open, completely exposed, and within range of a sniper's high-powered rifle.

"*Psssst!*" said a voice to her left. She looked and saw a small hand beckoning to her from the toilet door.

She ran for the cubicle, taking a last agonised look in Moss's direction as armed men surrounded him and Krishan.

14:28

"What the blimmin' heck is going on?" DC Patel demanded, seeing Arun, Donna and Sam crouching by the door of the disabled toilet.

"Shhh!" Donna said. "Can't you see? Like, duh!"

The door was open a crack and the children were peering out.

"Where's Dad?" Arun said.

"Those big dudes just took him and Mossy outside," said Donna.

"And what did the armed police do?"

"Nothing. They're toast."

"Can't we follow them?"

"Not yet. There's too many of them out there."

They watched through the gap as Thorne's three men emerged from the police station, broke into a jog past the police officers still writhing and groaning on the ground, and ran past the toilets to wait by the Terminus Place exit for their pick up.

"Come on, let's go," Arun said, grabbing his pack.

"Wait, where are you going?" Patel asked.

"After them, of course. They took my dad." Arun hurried out of the door with Donna close behind.

Sam shrugged as he pulled on his Iron Man backpack and said to Patel, "I know this sounds crazy, but you have to trust us. We know what we're doing."

"But – but you're just kids."

"Yeah, I know. Sick, isn't it?" Sam trotted out after his friends.

Patel dashed outside after him. "Wait! Come back!"

Four ambulances and six police cars screamed north up Buckingham Palace Road, past a black SUV heading in the opposite direction, away from Victoria and towards the Thames.

Thorne, sitting behind the driver, allowed himself a thin smile of satisfaction as the blue lights and wailing sirens flashed past.

"Everyone's clear," Lewis said. "And we've got Lal and Double-X too. Looks like you did it, sir."

He put his phone away and watched Thorne take the laptop out of its case and hit the power button.

"Almost," Thorne said. He reached into his suit and took out an aluminium cigar tube. Unscrewing the cap, he tipped out a human finger.

Lewis shrieked.

"It's not real, you idiot," Thorne said, holding it up. "It's Play-Doh. I got Krishan to put up some posters, using Blu-Tack. I was then able to take a blob of this and make an imprint, to capture his fingerprints in a three-dimensional model."

Thorne slid the putty over the fingerprint scanner.

There was a bleep and the words *Fingerprint accepted. Login initiated* appeared on screen.

"Genius," Lewis said.

Thorne sneered. "It was child's play. No pun intended."

Enter username and password popped up.

Thorne's fingers lightly tapped the keys and he sat back as he hit the return key.

"What?" he said, his smile vanishing like a popped bubble.

Password incorrect. Access denied. You have two more attempts was the on-screen message.

"I must have mistyped it," he said, keying in the name and password again, slowly and carefully tapping each letter.

Password incorrect. Access denied. You have one more attempt appeared on the screen.

"No!" Thorne slammed the lid shut. "He's changed the password."

"Who has?"

"Either Krishan or Double-X. It doesn't matter which. We have them both."

"What if they won't talk?"

"Then they'll be dead and we'll hack in anyway. I've come too far to let something like this stop me."

Confused tourists and commuters huddled round the main entrance to Victoria station, unsure of what to do or where to go.

The wail of emergency sirens grew louder and an ambulance skidded to a stop. A burly paramedic carrying a first-aid kit jumped out and ran through the crowd, shoving people aside as he made his way in.

He returned seconds later with two bruised and bloodied men, one with a diamond earring and the other a beanie hat. They climbed into the ambulance and it peeled away, siren blaring and blue lights flashing.

"That's them! They're getting away!" shouted Arun, pointing to the ambulance as Sam and DC Patel finally caught up with him and Donna outside the station.

"Oh no they're not," said Patel, pulling her car keys from her bag. "Come on!"

She stepped off the kerb and ran round a bus to where

she had parked the Audi. The children ran to catch up.

"Don't tell me that's yours," Donna said, pointing to a Westminster City Council vehicle removal truck that had just lifted a silver Audi on to its back for removal.

"Sorry, love," shouted the driver from the cab. "'S'what you get for parking on double yellow lines. See ya."

14:35

A white transit van barrelled west along Bayswater Road, towards Notting Hill. Sitting in the back, opposite each other on low benches, were Krishan Lal and DI Moss. Both had hoods over their heads, with their hands and feet cable-tied.

Krishan inched his feet to the left and right and felt them touch boots on either side. He could make out a low hissing sound that he recognised as music spilling from earbuds.

"Hey," he whispered, pitching his voice above the thrum of the engine and the rumble of the tyres on the road. "You, sitting opposite."

"Lal?" Moss whispered back. "Is that you?"

"Yes. Who are you and how'd you get into this mess?"

"The name's Moss. I'm a police officer. I'm here to help."

"Was getting captured part of your plan?"

"Uh, no."

"I see. So now what?"

"I don't know."

"That's great. Just great."

The van made a sharp left on to Holland Road, the movement tipping Krishan to the right. He fell against the man beside him who shoved him upright again.

"Krishan?" Moss whispered.

"What?"

"Don't give up. There are people out there ... working to free us."

"Who? Secret service?"

"And ... others. I can't say who, but if I were you, I wouldn't worry."

"If I were you, I would."

A pause. "Why's that?"

"These guys just shot four policemen but not you. Instead, they brought you along. Why?"

"I don't know."

"Exactly. Like I said, start worrying."

The man to Krishan's right elbowed him hard. "Shut it! No talking! That goes for both of you."

The van turned right, on to the A4, heading out of London.

DC Patel swore and kicked at the door of the flatbed lorry with a crane lift on its back, scuffing the words "City of

Westminster Authorised Removal Unit".

"Hey!" shouted the driver, opening the door and leaning out to check for a dent.

"Blooming Westminster fascist traffic wardens! I was only here five minutes!" Patel raged and kicked the door again.

"Oi! You stop that or I'll call the police!" said the driver.

"I *am* the police!" Patel said, brandishing her warrant card. "Give me back my car." She pointed at the Audi, its wheels secured by clamps and nylon straps.

"Yeah, and I'm David Beckham. Heard that one before, love."

Sam tracked the departing ambulance. "They're getting away," he said.

"Eh, mate, is something wrong?" said a man with a clipboard, coming round the rear of the removal lorry.

"Yeah, this lady's—"

"Stuff this." Patel put one foot on the large front tyre for height, stepped up to reach into the cab and grabbed the driver by his jacket collar. As she dropped down again, she yanked hard, sending the driver tumbling out of the cab and sprawling on to the tarmac.

"Kids, get in!" Patel commanded and climbed up into the cab, slamming the door and turning the ignition key. The engine roared into life.

Arun, Sam and Donna ran round to the passenger side, opened the door and bundled in.

Clipboard Man was coaxing the driver to his feet when DC Patel released the handbrake and stamped on the accelerator, sending the truck careening forward.

"Hey! That's my truck!" the driver yelled. "Someone call the police!"

"*I am the police!*" Patel shouted as the truck rumbled past and headed after the ambulance.

With its siren wailing and blue lights flashing, the ambulance surged on to Vauxhall Bridge Road, cutting across two lanes to follow the curve of the road south. Cars braked hard to allow the speeding ambulance through.

In the cab of the vehicle removal truck, Patel hit the hazard warning lights and sped up to join the traffic, as cars rushed towards her.

"Hang on," she said, heaving the large steering wheel.

Seeing that the ten-ton truck was not slowing, drivers hit their brakes, bringing their cars skidding to a stop as the truck cut in front of them. It clipped the nose of a Tesla, smashing the light and sending pieces of shattered plastic skipping along the asphalt. Horns blared as cars rear-ended one another.

The truck rounded the corner, its back end fishtailing as the squealing wheels spun to maintain grip. The ambulance was about twenty vehicles in front and pulling further ahead as cars gave way to let it through.

"Will we catch them in this heap?" Arun asked.

"This is London," Patel said. "They'll be lucky to do more than ten miles per hour."

"And can you drive this thing?" Donna asked, her knuckles white as she gripped the dashboard.

"I've done my Class 1 Advanced Driver's course."

"Advanced driving doesn't mean you can drive a truck," Donna said, her hands clawing for a seat belt.

"What's the plan?" Sam asked. "Apart from playing demolition derby?"

Patel spoke through gritted teeth, her eyes fixed on the road ahead. "If we can catch up with those guys, we can find out where the others are taking Andy – I mean DI Moss – and whatshisface."

"Hey, that 'whatshisface' is my dad," said Arun.

Patel slammed her hand down on the horn to warn off a red bus that was about to pull out. The ambulance was still a good distance in front.

"You know, we don't have to do this," Sam said. "We

don't have to chase them."

"Yes, we do," Patel said. "It's my job."

"No, really, there's another way we can—"

"If I want your input, I'll ask for it."

"We're too big and we're too slow," Arun said. "We're never going to catch them in this."

"Do you have a better idea?" Patel said, running through an amber light and thumping the horn. *BEE-BEEP!!*

Arun looked in the wing mirror and saw the Audi rocking on its wheels.

"Actually, I do," he said. "Sam, you still got your Swiss army knife?"

Sam nodded and fished a pocket knife from his blazer. "Here you go."

"Cheers." Arun took it and reached for the door handle. "Whatever you do, don't stop until I tell you."

"Wait! What are you doing?" Patel screamed as Arun opened the passenger door and climbed out.

14:42

The CITADEL boardroom was now a bustling emergency control centre, with various officials coordinating the multiple agencies summoned to assist with the ongoing crisis.

The minister ended his call and cleared his throat loudly. The room fell silent.

"Gentlemen, I've just had an update on the shooting incident at Victoria," he said. "It appears that our suspicions were correct and that the incident is linked."

"How can you be sure of that?" someone asked.

"A Transport Police officer heard the name 'Krishan Lal' and described a man of Lal's appearance being brought into the police station."

"Lal was at Victoria?"

"Yes. It seems that the kidnappers took him there for reasons unknown, before fleeing with him and a second hostage."

"That's a huge risk to take. Why bring him to the police only to take him away again? What are they thinking? And who is this second person?"

"Those are good questions. I'm hoping to get some answers very shortly. Secret Intelligence has a team on the way to Victoria right now. They'll sift through the CCTV footage and piece together the sequence of events."

"And until then?" General McAllister asked, raising an eyebrow.

"We wait."

"We wait? You mean to say key scientists go AWOL, a multibillion-pound project is in jeopardy, national security may well be compromised and all we can do is twiddle our thumbs?" the general said.

"I'm afraid so. Until we know who or what we are up against, we have to wait for their next move."

The pencil in McAllister's hand snapped. "All I can say is I hope to God that someone is showing a darned sight more initiative than we are. Otherwise this will not end well."

Stepping out of a moving vehicle is never a good idea, Arun reflected. It's an even worse idea when that vehicle is a heavy truck moving at thirty miles per hour through London traffic, constantly swerving and changing lanes.

He pushed open the cab door and, gripping the seat belt in his left hand, he placed his left foot on the wheel

147

arch and swung out, pivoting on his tiptoes so that his chest pressed against the cab. His right hand grabbed for the bars of the metal cage that protected the crane machinery and his right foot stretched to brace against the edge of the flatbed of the truck.

Donna's eyes bulged and she swore under her breath.

"This isn't Mad Max!" DC Patel shrieked. "Get back in here!"

Arun clung spread-eagled against the side of the cab and shook his head.

"I'm going to stop this truck right now if you don't get back inside," Patel shouted. "I mean it."

"If you do that, they'll get away," Sam said.

"Was I talking to you?" Patel snapped.

Donna held the door open and shouted, "Arun, are you out of your freaking mind?" She looked back at Patel and said, "He's OK. He's got a good grip. Just keep driving – I'll watch out for him."

"And what are you going to do if he falls? Catch him? I don't want that on my conscience," Patel said.

"Arun won't fall. He's school champion at free climbing," Sam lied. "He knows what he's doing."

Patel took a last look at Arun in the wing mirror. He managed to give her a thumbs-up signal.

"All right," she muttered, "but I don't like this one bit."

"Just don't lose them," Sam said, pointing at the ambulance ahead.

Arun closed his eyes and felt the wind whipping his hair and tugging his blazer. His limbs were stiff with terror.

"What are you doing, you stupid kid?" shouted a driver, who gaped at the schoolboy hanging off the side as the truck cruised past.

Arun let go of the seat belt and pushed himself away towards the flatbed, bringing both hands on to the bars of the equipment cage.

Inside the cab, Sam shrank into his seat as Patel weaved in and out of the two lanes of traffic, her horn blaring. She checked the wing mirror to see that Arun was still clinging to the truck.

"Hang on," she said, and yanked the wheel sharply to the right, sending the truck over the white lines into the opposite lane and a 200-metre stretch free of oncoming cars.

"Look out for the island!" Sam shouted.

The front wheel clipped the kerb of a traffic island, jarring the truck, which bounced over it and on through a plastic bollard, sending it somersaulting across the road.

As the truck bucked the kerb, Arun was jolted upwards and the passenger door swung wide open, with Donna still holding on to it.

"*Heeelp!*" she screamed as she slid out.

Sam grabbed at her shirt to save her and dug his fingers into the back of his seat to steady himself.

Arun kept both hands glued to the bars but, as his feet came down, they missed the edge of the flatbed, and plunged towards the blur of speeding asphalt below.

His left shoe scraped the tarmac for a second while his right foot brushed something solid as it fell. Arun instinctively kicked up for it, touching down on a solid metal rail. He brought his trailing leg up and, once he had both feet on the safety bar that ran down the side of the truck, he straightened up.

Now that the truck had an open stretch of road, Patel dropped the gears and pressed the accelerator to the floor. The engine groaned and the truck blazed past car after car on the left, closing in on the ambulance.

The ambulance driver looked in his wing mirror and saw a Westminster City Council vehicle removal truck driving up the wrong side of the road.

"Hey, fellas!" he said. "Take a look out of the back window and tell me if you're seein' what I'm seein'."

The two bruisers in the back of the speeding ambulance

peered through the rear smoked-glass window.

"Someone's in an awful hurry," said Earring Man, still nursing his broken nose.

"That's right," said Beanie. "Are they following us?"

"It sure looks that way," Earring Man said, his eyes narrowing.

"Not for long," Beanie said, drawing his pistol.

Donna slammed the door shut and wound the window down so she could lean out and watch Arun. Sam looked up and squealed. The traffic was moving again on this side of the road and a red double-decker was fast approaching.

"There's a bus coming!" Sam said, his voice rising.

"I see it," Patel said, looking for a gap on the left.

"It's getting closer."

"I can see that."

"We're on the wrong side."

"I know."

"It's going to—"

The bus's horn blared and the driver stamped on the brakes, leaving tyre marks behind as the big truck thundered towards him.

"Arun! Hold on!" Donna screamed.

14:46

A space opened up on the left. DC Patel slammed on the brakes and cranked the steering wheel, aiming for the gap. The back end of the truck slid outwards into the path of the oncoming bus. With a smash, the front of the bus clipped the rear of the truck, shoving it aside. Arun was jolted again, but this time his footing was sound.

The ambulance was now only four cars in front, still picking its way through the traffic.

Arun clambered up on to the flatbed of the truck. Four nylon tethers stretched from the gantry of the crane down to grabs round each wheel, holding the car in place.

Gripping a strap for balance, Arun tugged at the nearest tyre grab, an A-shaped piece of metal with steel shafts jutting backwards, but it would not move; there was no slack in the tether.

He fished out Sam's pocket knife, opened the blade with his teeth and began to saw at the strap. At first it was hard going – the sharp blade seemed to have no effect as he furiously worked it back and forth – but once the blade finally bit, the tension in the strap pulled at the two sides of the cut and it became easier.

When he cut the final strands, the wheel grab clunked to the metal deck while the strap whipped upwards to flap in the breeze. Arun slid the grab aside, took hold of the door handle for support and moved over to free up the next wheel.

"We're gaining on them!" Sam said, bouncing up and down in his seat.

"Yeah," DC Patel said, her eyes fixed on the ambulance ahead. "Donna, what's your friend doing back there? I can't see him any more. Did he fall off?"

Donna, who was leaning out of her window and looking back at Arun, grinned. She pushed long wisps of hair out of her face and said, "Believe me, you don't want to know." She ducked over to where Patel's handbag lay on the cab floor near her feet, and pulled out a bunch of car keys.

"What do you want to do?" the ambulance driver said, overtaking a black cab. "We can outrun them easy enough."

"Yeah," Earring Man said, "but that doesn't stop them clocking our registration or telling someone where we are or where we're headed."

"Dead men make poor witnesses," Beanie said from the back, waving his Browning pistol.

"Slow down. Let them think they're catching up. Bring them in close." Earring Man handed a police sub-machine gun to his fellow soldier. "Soon as we make the left turn, we hit 'em high and low. Finish them off."

"It'll be my pleasure," Beanie said, slipping off the safety catch.

The second wheel grab thudded to the deck, and Arun dropped on all fours to slide on his front under the Audi to its other side. He emerged by the rear driver's-side wheel, his white shirt now grubby, and set to cutting the third nylon strap.

Horn blaring, DC Patel swung the truck across two lanes into a gap and then out again, all the time gaining on the ambulance.

"They're not getting away from me," she said, leaning over the steering wheel as if ready to climb through the windscreen.

"I don't like it," said Sam.

"You don't like anything," Patel snapped.

"But we shouldn't be able to catch them in this wreck. You said it yourself."

"Maybe I'm a better driver than you thought."

"That, or they're slowing down."

"And letting us catch them? Why would they do that?"

Sam shrugged. "I don't know, but these guys aren't stupid."

"They're criminal scumbags. Of course they're stupid."

Donna and Sam exchanged looks of growing alarm.

Arun held on to the driver's door handle with one hand, while the knife in his other cut through the final strands of fibre holding the last tyre grab. It fell away and he allowed himself a small smile.

The sound of an electronic chirp made him jump. The indicator lights flashed and the car doors unlocked as Donna, watching him through the wing mirror, hit the remote on the key fob.

"Left turn coming up," the ambulance driver said, his voice rising.

"We're ready!" Beanie said, cradling the H & K carbine.

Earring Man, crouching next to him in the back, chambered a round into his Browning and grinned.

* * *

The road ahead widened as the junction with John Islip Street approached on the left.

The ambulance was in the offside lane, hugging the middle of the road, and sped towards the junction.

"They're going straight, towards Vauxhall Bridge," Patel said, and floored the accelerator.

Standing beside the Audi on the back of the truck, Arun saw that the ambulance was now only twenty metres in front. The truck engine roared and coughed out a puff of black smoke as it picked up more speed.

Arun, feeling the wind whipping through his slim frame and the juddering of the truck's suspension, took this as his cue to get into the car. He opened the door of the Audi, slipped into the front seat and fastened his seat belt.

This small action, so practised and familiar, made him feel foolish. Here he was, a twelve-year-old boy sitting in the driver's seat of an unmarked police car, stuck on the back of a truck as it hurtled across London chasing kidnappers. What had he been thinking? It wasn't as if he had thought to bring the car keys with him and, even if he had, what would he do with them? It wasn't like he could drive and, supposing he could, how was he meant to know—

He snapped out of his reverie as the truck skewed to the left so sharply that two side wheels lifted off the ground. The Audi, now untethered, began to slide across the back of the truck, as the centrifugal force of the turn pushed it nearer to the edge.

Arun grabbed the steering wheel and screamed.

At the last moment the ambulance had cut across the outside lane, skidding into a sharp left turn on to John Islip Street.

Patel swore and floored the brake while spinning the steering wheel hard to the left. The truck tyres squealed in protest and the heavy vehicle slewed across the junction, its rear sliding out, slowing and leaving dirty snakes of mangled rubber on the asphalt. As the truck fishtailed across the junction, two men kicked open the back doors of the ambulance and opened fire, one with a sub-machine gun – *BRAAAAAAP!!* – strafing the front of the truck, and the other with a handgun – *POOM!-POOM!-POOM!* – emptying the entire magazine into the cab, punching spiderwebbed fractures across the windscreen.

The front glass of the cab shattered, screams filled the tiny space and blood spattered across the inside.

14:51

Quinn rested one knee on the floor of Victoria station concourse and picked up a hardened black rubber ball the size of a gobstopper. He stood up, turned in a circle and scanned the array of now deserted shops and food outlets, his eyes coming to rest on a large electronic hoarding, its display changing to a poster advertising holidays to Disneyland.

"There," he said to his team. "Sniper would have been behind there. You, go and check for shell casings in case they had to leave in a hurry."

An agent trotted off in the direction of the poster.

Two other members of Quinn's team approached from the Transport Police station, leading a trembling Japanese girl and a Transport Police officer.

"You're not police—" the officer started to say.

"Shut it. I ask the questions, not you," Quinn said. He snapped his fingers and an agent handed him a manila envelope. Quinn pulled out a stack of photographs, selected one and thrust it under the policeman's nose.

"Who's this?" Quinn said.

"That's the chap who came in half an hour ago. Had two big fellas with him."

Quinn raised an eyebrow. "Go on."

"He was a bit beat-up looking. Had a cut over his eye here." The officer drew a finger above his left brow. "But no worse than some of what you see round here."

"Did you get this man's name?"

"Yeah. Lal. Something like that. Krishan Lal. Another man came in, shouted his name and then it all kicked off."

"Who was this other man?"

The officer shrugged. "Said he was police."

"Police?" Quinn spat out the word.

"Gaffer, you thinking what I'm thinking?" Green said.

Quinn grimaced. "Yeah. Who'd have thought DI Moss was in on it the whole time? And there he was, listening in on us. No wonder the kidnappers didn't phone. He must've nicked the spare laptop too."

Taking the policeman to one side, Quinn lowered his voice and said, "Did you see any kids around? Two boys and a girl, probably in school uniform?"

"Huh? No. Why?"

"I'm asking the questions, not you."

Brown walked up with a hard drive in his hand. "Here's

all the CCTV footage."

"All right. Let's get back to base and go through this properly," Quinn said, checking his watch. "I've got to give an update in ten minutes."

The storm of bullets punched through the truck's cab, smashing the headlights and pockmarking the front panel.

Beanie emptied the sub-machine gun in seconds, spraying fire in a diagonal arc that swept from the Renault symbol down to the front driver-side tyre. The tyre exploded with a bang and the weight of the truck crashed down on the alloy hub, shredding the rubber and sending up a fountain of sparks.

Inside the cab, DC Patel felt a searing pain in her left arm and the truck began to reel out of control. She gripped the wheel with all her strength, straining to control the skid, but she couldn't see anything through the mosaic of a windscreen. She felt Donna's weight pull down on the wheel beside her and the two of them clung on.

Beanie grinned as the truck spun, and pulled the ambulance doors shut.

"Job done!" he said, and high-fived his partner. "Let's go!"

Inside the Audi, Arun's stomach heaved as he felt the car begin to judder and slide across the metal deck towards the edge of the flatbed. As his mind was registering this, he heard the staccato sound of gunfire and saw daylight appear through several holes in the back of the cab. There was a sickening lurch as the truck pitched forward and careened across the junction, its rear sliding into the other lane.

Arun was dizzied by the buildings spinning around him and was dimly aware that the truck was in danger of tipping over, with him stuck on its back, so he did the only thing he could think of: he waited for the spin to slow, took a deep breath – and released the handbrake.

The back of the truck swung like the second hand of a clock, sweeping out in a wide curve across the junction while Patel and Donna clung to the steering wheel to keep the front wheels turned into the skid – otherwise the truck would overturn. The screech of protesting tyres filled their ears and they kept their eyes and teeth clamped shut, not daring to look, just praying for the truck to stop its slide.

As the truck spun round, its front coming to face the opposite direction and its rear swinging with it, the Audi launched off the back platform like a fighter jet taking off from an aircraft carrier, hurtling backwards with all the speed of the skidding truck. Arun screamed again and felt his stomach heave as the car sailed through the air towards the uprushing tarmac. There was a tremendous jolt and Arun would have slammed into the ceiling were it not for the seat belt locking him down.

The car bounced on two wheels, then on four, and Arun had enough sense left to stamp the brake pedal to the floor, bringing the Audi to a screeching tyre-smearing stop. Blood pounded in his ears and he looked up to see the stricken truck in front of him.

He opened the car door, fighting down the urge to be sick and stepped out to find his legs had turned to jelly. The stench of burnt rubber filled the air.

Passers-by stopped and stared, open-mouthed. Traffic continued to whizz by on the Vauxhall Bridge Road behind and cars had stopped on both sides of John Islip Street, their path blocked by the crippled truck.

The cab doors opened slowly and Patel climbed down first, her left sleeve slick with blood. Donna stepped out after her and took her right arm. Sam tumbled out of the passenger side, his round face so pale that it reflected back the spring sunshine.

Sam caught up with Patel and said, "I told you those guys weren't stupid."

"You don't have many friends, do you?" she said through gritted teeth.

"Hey, you can't leave that truck there!" a stalled cabbie shouted as the battered trio passed his taxi.

"Someone call the police!" another shouted.

"*I am the police!*" Patel yelled back.

They hobbled up to the Audi and Patel looked at Arun, her head cocked to one side.

"Did you just drive my car off the truck and land it here?" she said.

Arun nodded.

"Did you mean to do that?"

Arun shook his head.

Patel looked from the car to the wrecked truck. "Wow. I didn't know it could do that."

"So now what?" Donna said, ignoring the growing crowd of onlookers.

"Uh, they're still getting away," Sam said, his hand shielding his eyes from the sun as he watched the ambulance make a right on to Ponsonby Place.

"The heck they are," Patel said, wincing as she reached for the car door.

"Uh-uh," Donna said. "No way you're driving, not with one arm. I'll drive."

"Let me drive," Sam said.

"You can't drive," Arun, Patel and Donna said together.

"Yeah, I can," Sam said.

"What have you driven?" Donna asked.

"Uh, *Grand Theft Auto*," Sam said, finding the scuff marks on his shoes to be of great interest.

"That settles it," Donna said. "I'm driving. Officer, you get in the back with Sam. Arun, in front with me."

No one dared argue. Five seconds later, Donna had adjusted the driver's seat, lowered the steering column and turned the key in the ignition. She stepped on the clutch, slid the gear stick into first and pressed down on the accelerator, keeping her left hand on the brake lever. The engine roared and the rear tyres spun, howling in rage and sending up a black cloud of burning rubber. The rpm needle climbed into the red and the car started to shudder.

"Hang on to your pants," Donna said, releasing the handbrake.

The car leaped forward like a coiled cheetah bounding after its prey and roared down the street towards the junction with Ponsonby Place.

Donna slipped through the gears in seconds and the speedometer needle jumped to 50 miles per hour.

Arun cringed as he saw cars moving across the road ahead, oblivious to the slab of metal speeding towards them.

"Red light, red light!" he said, his voice rising with each word.

Donna flipped the dashboard switch, flicking on the flashing blue lights hidden behind the radiator grille, and sounding the police siren. *WOW-WOW-WOW-WOW!*

The Audi rushed towards the two rows of moving cars and Donna's hands and feet were a blur as she dropped into second gear, spun the power steering and pulled up on the handbrake as the car reached the junction.

Arun covered his eyes as the Audi sliced between a cement mixer and a removals van, skidded in front of a bus, cut inside a heavy goods lorry and shot out again, surging down the centre line, sending cars over to each side.

"*Yeee-haaah!*" Donna whooped in delight. "Let's go kick some butt!"

Arun leaned out of the window and heaved, about to throw up.

"No! You'll mess up my car!" Patel said.

"Here, use this!" Sam said, pulling an empty sandwich bag from his backpack.

"Thanks," Arun said, his face green. He pressed the opening to his lips and erupted.

"Oh, that is so rank!" Donna said, putting a hand over her nose.

"Keep both hands on the wheel!" Patel screamed.

Earring Man, squatting in the back of the ambulance, was the first to hear the siren. He tilted his head and made a face. "Is our siren still on?" he asked the driver.

"No. I killed it a while back."

"Then what am I hearing?"

The driver looked in his mirror. "Aw, no!" he said. "I don't freakin' believe it! It's the police!"

Earring Man looked back. "It's not the police," he spat. "It's them."

14:55

Captain Ian Whitby of the Royal Marines Fleet Protection Group strode into the MANDROID Command Bunker. The Marines on duty snapped to attention at their workstations and saluted.

"At ease," Whitby said, and he made his way to the main desk, opposite a huge window overlooking a brightly lit aircraft hangar.

Lieutenant Simon Burgess, his second-in-command, handed him a red telephone receiver: the secure line from Whitehall.

"Whitby here," he said into the phone.

Burgess watched his captain closely, trying to read him for clues as to why the MOD top brass was calling.

"Yes, Major, if that is what you wish," Whitby said, before putting down the phone.

"Sir?" Burgess said.

"We've been put on a state of high alert," Whitby said, sounding bemused. "Seems like some terrorist group is looking to target an MOD site."

"Why call us? We don't officially exist, so how can we be a target?"

Whitby shrugged. "I'm not privy to how these decisions are made. All I know is that we've been ordered to go to Amber Alert and to double all patrols."

"What a waste of time that'll be."

Whitby gazed out into the hangar. The only vehicle in it was a large motor home, which was surrounded by a team of technicians wearing lab coats and holding clipboards.

"Let's hope so," he said. "I watched the last test of that thing, after the mods were made and, believe me, you don't want it falling into the wrong hands."

On the south bank of the River Thames, on the Albert Embankment beside Vauxhall Bridge, lie the headquarters of the British Secret Intelligence Service. Deep within the building, Special Agent Quinn knocked on a heavy oak door and entered the office of "C", the chief of the SIS.

C was sitting behind a large desk, reading through a sheaf of papers. He looked up over his half-moon spectacles and gestured for Quinn to take a seat.

He read on for a few minutes, before leaning back in his chair. "Bit of a pickle this."

"That's one way of putting it, sir," said Quinn.

"What's your assessment?"

"My assessment? That this chap Thorne knows enough about the MANDROID programme to steal the prototype."

"You think he's able to do it?"

"Yes, sir, I do."

C leaned forward. "You understand that cannot be allowed to happen, under any circumstances?"

"I do, sir."

C stood up and went to a side table that held two crystal tumblers and a decanter on a silver tray. He poured measures of malt whisky into the two glasses and handed one to Quinn.

"How long have you been with the Service, Quinn? Is it twenty-five years?"

"Thirty-two, sir. Plus six months and eighteen days, but who's counting?"

C sighed. "It was so much simpler back then. You knew who the enemy was, what you had to do. Now, though... Have you read the MANDROID file?"

"I have, sir."

C nodded. "You know my first thought when I read it?"

"This can't be real?"

C chuckled. "After that. My second thought was 'Trinity'."

"Sir?"

"It may be before your time. 16 July 1945. Alamogordo, New Mexico. No? The world's first atomic bomb test. *Trinity* was the code name. One new weapon and the world changed overnight."

"Sir, are you saying that Project MANDROID could be … on the same lines?"

"What I'm saying is that in the wrong hands it has the potential to start World War Three."

"Isn't that a bit—"

"What, melodramatic? You've read the report. You know what it can do." C fixed his steady gaze on Quinn.

"So … what would be our preferred endgame?" Quinn asked.

"Ideally I'd prefer it if the MANDROID was taken out of MOD control and put beyond their reach. It's bad enough they encouraged Thorne to weaponise it. I don't trust politicians to resist the temptation to use it militarily. That's not what it was designed for. The question is, can we do this?"

Quinn nodded. "Yes. I have an idea, sir. It's a bit left field, but you're going to have to trust me."

"I'm listening."

Quinn reached into his jacket and pulled out three dossiers, which he placed on the desk. The names *Arun Lal*, *Sam Evans* and *Donna Critchlow* were printed on the covers.

C leaned over, opened the top one and raised an eyebrow towards Quinn.

"Are these—"

"Yes, sir. They're perfect. Completely off the grid. No one knows about them. And, since they're just kids, they'll be easy to control."

"You want to take a game-changing device like MANDROID and put it in the hands of children? That's more than left field – it's off the reservation."

"Read the files, sir. One of those kids has an IQ of 208."

C let out a low whistle and sat down. He studied Quinn carefully. "I thought you hated kids."

"I do," Quinn said, "but I know an asset when I see one."

"If you seriously think you can pull this off, then I'll go with it. Otherwise I want the MANDROID completely destroyed."

"Understood, sir."

The silver Audi weaved in and out of the traffic like a barracuda swimming through a pod of whales. The flashing lights and police siren parted the two lines of traffic ahead of them.

A sheen of sweat glistened on Donna's brow as she concentrated on the road, one hand constantly ramming the gear stick back and forth, the other spinning the steering wheel to claim space as it appeared.

Arun vomited again, wiped his mouth on the sleeve of his blazer and tied a knot in the neck of the sandwich bag, which was now the size of a small football.

"That's what you get for eating Marmite," Donna said, her eyes fixed on the ambulance ahead.

"Can we find a bin?" Arun said weakly.

"I'm not stopping, so you'd better hang on to it."

Patel winced as Donna slammed the car into another lane and her shoulder hit the door. She reached a hand inside her jacket and drew it out, her fingers slick with fresh blood.

"Arun," she said, "there's a first-aid kit under your seat. Can you pass it back to Sam?"

"How bad is it?" Sam asked, taking the green box from Arun.

"Just a flesh wound," Patel said. "I'm lucky. It missed the bone and went through."

"You call that lucky?" Sam said.

"Oh, yeah. Another fifteen centimetres in and it would've been my heart. I had worse than this when I walked the beat."

"Why are they gaining on us?" Earring Man asked the ambulance driver. "Can't you shake them off?"

"What do you think I'm trying to do?" the driver shouted, overtaking a delivery van. "They're faster than we are and the little one is a heck of a driver."

"Little one?"

"The one driving. Take a look. All I can see is a small head bobbing up and down."

Donna dropped a gear as a gap opened up between cars and floored the accelerator. The wheels spun for a moment before regaining traction and the Audi lurched forward through the space, its engine roaring in triumph.

The ambulance loomed up in the windscreen, weaving from side to side.

Beanie tossed away the empty H & K MP5 and unholstered his Browning. He grabbed the back of the driver's seat to steady himself and thrust his face forward.

"Gimme your gun," he said.

The driver handed his pistol over.

"They still behind us?" Earring Man asked, slapping a new clip into his Browning.

"Yeah," the driver shouted, after checking his mirror.

Earring Man grinned, a pistol in each hand. "I'll count three, then we let 'em have it – both barrels, same as before. Go for the driver this time."

"Got it," Beanie said, his thumb sliding off the safety catch.

The red brake lights of the ambulance in front lit up for a moment as it slowed slightly and stopped its zig-zagging across the two lanes.

"Uh-oh," said Sam.

"One," said Earring Man, bracing himself against a fire extinguisher, guns at the ready.

"Fool me once, shame on you..." Donna muttered through clenched teeth as she closed in on the ambulance.

"Two," Earring Man said, raising a boot to kick open the doors.

* * *

"Fool me twice, shame on me," Donna finished, downshifting two gears, wrenching the wheel to the right and stamping hard on the right-hand pedal.

"Three!" Earring Man kicked open the ambulance's rear doors, and he and his partner opened fire. *BLAM! POW! P-TING!* Several rounds chewed into the tarmac, narrowly missing a Smart car some ten metres behind.

"Where have they gone?" Beanie bellowed.

Donna felt herself thrown back into her seat as the Audi blitzed alongside the ambulance, two wheels over the central white line.

There was a loud blare of a horn as a red bus came directly towards them. Donna jerked the steering to the left, willing the car to suck in its sides. There was a crack as the driver-side wing mirror sheared off and the whole right side was thrown into shadow as the bus thundered past, so close that Donna could have reached out and kissed it.

Then suddenly the bus was gone, far behind, and the ambulance was falling away on the left. Donna pressed the button for the passenger window, opening Arun's side. She tapped his leg and jerked a thumb towards the window. Arun didn't know how, but he understood what she meant.

Four hundred metres ahead a broken-down bus had pulled over, its hazard lights blinking.

"They're in front of us!" the ambulance driver said, pointing at the Audi.

Earring Man scrambled to the front of the vehicle and levelled his two pistols. "Stay with 'em!"

"Don't shoot next to my ear!" the driver said, pressing himself against the door. "And I need my windscreen intact to see where I'm going, you idiot!"

"No witnesses, remember?" The soldier's fingers tightened on the triggers as he took aim at the police car.

"Wait! What's that?" Beanie said, pointing as a plastic bag flew out of the Audi's passenger window, its blobby shape twisting and stretching as it swept through the air at fifty miles per hour, like a giant drop of water.

SPLAT! It hit the front windscreen of the ambulance and exploded, splattering lumpy brown slop across the glass, as if a bucket of soup had been emptied from a great height.

"I can't see! I can't see!" the driver screamed, searching for the windscreen wipers.

WHAMM! The ambulance smashed into the back of the stalled bus and tore through its rear section, crumpling metal and shattering glass.

Donna brought the car to a screeching stop and looked in the rear-view mirror, hand over her mouth.

Without a word Patel got out and walked towards the wreckage. Onlookers shied away as she approached. She went round to the back of the bus and looked inside the crumpled remains of the ambulance.

"He-help!" said a voice from the driver's seat. "Call ... the police..."

Patel looked around inside and picked up a loose handgun and a walkie-talkie. "I am the police," she said. "Where are the two men you took from Victoria? Lal and Moss?"

"Call ... me ... an ambulance... Promise me..."

"Sure – *after* you tell me where you've taken those prisoners." Patel's nostrils were flared and her voice was low.

"I ... don't have to ... tell you ... nothing..." the driver spat in her direction. "I know my rights... Now ... call me an ambulance..."

Patel's lip twisted in anger. "Fine. You're an ambulance."

She slammed the door and strode back to the Audi.

"You," she said to a gawking pedestrian, "call 999. Tell them you need all three emergency services and that it's related to the incident at Victoria. Cheers."

She reached the Audi and looked in through the open window. "Donna, you're right. You *can* drive."

"Are they...?" Donna whispered.

"They're a mess but they'll live," Patel said.

"So, Detective, what now?" Arun asked.

Patel's shoulders sagged. "Call me Sunny. And I don't know," she said. "They're not going to be telling us anything. Guess that's the end of the road."

Arun beamed at her. "Maybe not," he said. "What if I said we know where they were going?"

Sunny looked at him in disbelief. "Then I'd say, 'Let's go before my colleagues show up and start asking awkward questions.'"

"Better get in then."

Sunny jumped back into her seat, next to Sam who was checking his iPhone.

"They're on the M25, heading south, just past Junction 14," he said, squinting at the screen.

"You're tracking them?" Sunny said.

Sam smiled.

"You do know you're just kids, right?"

Sam winked. "Yeah, sick isn't it?"

"You'd better tell me everything."

Donna started the engine and the Audi pulled away as the sound of sirens came closer.

15:27

Donna signalled before changing lanes to avoid the exit for Heathrow Airport.

"Keep going down to Junction 12, then pick up the M3 towards Southampton," Sam said, his eyes on his phone.

"Gotcha," Donna said, as they passed Junction 14 on the M25.

Sunny ran a finger along the inside edge of the bandage round her left arm, to loosen it. She rotated her shoulder, her face twisting with pain.

"You should let it rest," Sam said, "before you start it bleeding again."

"Yeah, yeah, whatever," she said, leaning back and closing her eyes. "You know, there's still a few things I don't get."

"Such as?" Arun said, resting his arm on the back of his seat and twisting round.

"You're able to track them, so why did we just go and chase those idiots across London?"

"You wanted to. Said it was your job, remember? We tried to tell you."

"OK, I'll give you that. But you got Thorne to take your dad to Victoria, right?"

"Correct."

"What were you thinking? I mean, Transport Police?"

"It's a kidnapping," Arun said. "What else do we do? Doesn't a kidnapping end when the hostage is safe in police hands? At least, that's what I thought. We were kind of making it up as we went along, you know."

"Yeah, I got that bit. And what's with giving over the laptop? I know it's blank and all, but why let them think they got what they want? That's hardly going to slow them down, is it?"

"We didn't have much choice: we had to bargain with something for Dad. How was I to know the police would be so stupid as to hand him right back?" Arun's face reddened as anger surged in him.

Sunny opened her eyes. "It wasn't that simple. You had professional soldiers up against a volunteer constable. What chance did he have?"

"What chance did Dad have? At least your guys have training. All they had to do was take Dad in and this would have all been over."

"Arun, you're a clever boy, so why don't you shut up and think before you say anything else?"

Arun's cheeks felt hot and flushed, stung by the words.

"This isn't a dumb computer game where you win by achieving a set goal," Sunny went on. "This is real life and these guys we're up against aren't stupid." She shot a look at Sam. "They're organised, they're armed and they've got a plan. What makes you think a few silly kids getting in way over their heads is going to make any difference to them? The only reason you're still alive is that they don't know you exist."

Arun blinked back hot stinging tears and slumped in his seat.

Donna sucked her teeth, flicked the indicator downwards and swung the car across four lanes, neatly slipping between two lorries and braking hard once she reached the hard shoulder.

"What are you doing?" Sunny shouted as the car lurched to a stop and Donna killed the engine.

Donna whirled round in her seat. "You're lucky I'm driving, else I'd get out and slap you," she said, meaning every word.

"I beg your pardon?" Sunny said.

"Listen up, and listen good. Every time the feds have got involved, you know what's happened? You've got your butts kicked, that's what. Back at Arun's house, you were there and you went and sat in the car, meaning we were the ones who snuck in, past these MI6 bad boys, and got hold of the laptop. We were the ones who jacked the security on it, smuggled it out and copied all the data. What were you doing? Nothing. We were the ones who got Thorne to the meeting point and we gave him the laptop so we could track him with it. When Mossy showed up, all he did was get himself caught and now we have to save his sorry backside too."

Sam decided at that moment that he was in love.

"Let me ask you a question," Donna continued.

Sunny had both eyebrows raised and the trace of a smile was playing around her lips. "OK."

"Without us, what would you have right now?"

Sunny stopped to consider the question. After a long pause, she said, "Nothing. Absolutely nothing."

"Which sort of makes you a defective detective, doesn't it?" Sam offered.

"I rest my case," Donna said. "So, you wanna get out and hitch a lift home or are you gonna start to believe? Just because your boyfriend got busted, don't take it out on us."

Sunny stared and her mouth opened and closed like a landed fish. "How – How did you know about that?"

Donna rolled her eyes. "Give it up. Why is it people who are seeing each other always think they're being so clever at keeping it from everyone else? It's obvious! I can see it in the way you look at him. So, what's it gonna be?"

Sunny shook her head slowly. "You're right. I've underestimated you, all of you. I'm sorry for what I said. Now, can we get moving again before highway police stop and ask why a child is driving?"

"All right," Donna said, and she restarted the engine. "Just fix your attitude and give us some respect."

The Audi picked up speed once more and merged with the southbound traffic.

Tyres crunched on gravel as the black SUV pulled up outside a thatched farm cottage wreathed with pink climbing roses. It drove round the house to the barns at the back and parked between a Jeep and a white transit van. A number of other vehicles were parked there too.

The passenger doors opened and Galahad Thorne stepped out. He went into the nearest barn where a group of some twenty mercenaries snapped to attention. One of them, a lanky individual wearing a mannequin mask, glided over.

"Hello, Galahad," Saipher said.

"Is everyone here?" Thorne asked.

"All apart from Team Four."

"The ambulance?"

"Yes. They were the last to leave."

"Making them the last to arrive."

"Shall we wait for them?"

Thorne checked his watch. "No, not with the traffic at this hour. They miss the rendezvous, they miss the pay cheque. Not my problem. We continue as planned."

Lewis ended the call he was on and waved his mobile at Thorne.

"Sir, the transport's on its way."

"OK, you all know what to do. Let's go."

15:58

Quinn stepped out of the Range Rover and surveyed the crash scene. He kneeled to touch two long black smears streaking away along the asphalt surface.

With his team in close attendance, he followed the tyre tracks back to the bus, before stopping to assess the wreckage of the ambulance embedded in the lower deck.

"Good thing they called us in," Quinn said. "Looks like someone overtook the ambulance and forced it into this lane."

"Yeah," Green agreed. "Witnesses say it all happened very quickly."

"A silver Audi?"

"Yep. Licence plate is—"

Quinn continued to assess the crash site. "Richmond CID."

"How did you kno—"

"It's Moss's car; it was parked outside the Lal home this morning." Quinn sighed. "OK, so Moss escapes with Lal in a white transit, while these jokers make their own way from Victoria, until the Audi ruins their day. Question number one: who's driving the Audi?"

Green consulted his notebook. "Witnesses say an Asian woman got out. Medium height and build, shoulder-length hair, wearing a trouser suit."

"That'd be DC Patel, also at the house earlier. Question number two: why would she want to stop the ambulance?"

"She doesn't know Moss is one of the kidnappers?"

"Possibly. Or she's in on it too. Three men down means three less to split the ransom with. Where's that car now?"

"ANPR cameras logged it heading out of London at three o'clock. We've got local plod watching out but it's not a priority for them."

"Make it a priority."

Quinn walked round the bus towards the crumpled remains of the ambulance. A forensics team in white bunny-suit coveralls was picking through the wreckage.

"Any fingerprints?" Quinn called over to the nearest technician, who was dusting purple powder over the inside with a fine brush.

"Too many," was the reply. "There are hundreds, and most of them overlap. Looks like this was a normal ambulance before your suspects got their mitts on it."

Quinn checked his watch. "Do you know where the

casualties were taken?"

"St Thomas's Hospital. But they're going to be in theatre a while judging by the state they were in."

Quinn turned away and saw a forensics technician climb out of the bus, holding a test tube in a ziplock bag. His eyes zeroed in on the bag. "What've you got there?" he called.

"It's a-a ... some compound that was on the windscreen," the man stammered. "Witnesses say it, uh, impaired driver visibility and, um, caused the ambulance to crash."

Quinn reached out a hand. "Let me see that."

The technician shrank back. "It's evidence! We need to run toxicology reports, chemical analyses, lab checks—"

"You'll be getting a dental check in a minute. Hand it over!" Quinn snatched the bag, opened it and examined the sticky brown goo in the test tube.

"Looks like puke," Green said, peering over Quinn's shoulder. "Or diarrhoea."

"There's one way to check." Quinn unscrewed the plastic cap and sniffed at the contents. He recoiled as if slapped in the face and gagged. "It's puke, all right," he said, handing the bag back to the forensics technician. "I've just saved you a lab test. You can bill me later."

"Someone threw a bag of spew over the window?"

Green said, his face twisted in disgust. "That's sick!"

"Yeah, but it worked," Quinn muttered.

Green's mobile buzzed. "Gaffer, they've ID'd the ambulance driver."

"And?"

"He's dead."

"He's what? I thought his airbag went off and—"

"No. He's been officially dead for over two years. MOD report says he died in a helicopter crash in Afghanistan. Served with British Special Forces."

Quinn ran a hand over his face and took a deep breath. "Oh my word," he said. "That explains it. Get me everything you can on that crash. I want the names of everyone on board that chopper, full service histories, dossiers, medical records, the lot – and I want it now!"

"They're moving again," Sam said from his seat behind Donna. "I thought they'd maybe stopped for good in Newnham but it looks like it was just a rest stop."

"Where are they going now?" Donna asked, her eyes on the road ahead.

"Heading south towards the A30."

"You can see all that on your phone?" Sunny asked.

Sam nodded. "Right now, they're on Ridge Lane."

Sunny leaned over to see the iPhone screen. "Tell me how you're doing that," she said. "Please."

"It's really simple," Sam said. "I stashed a GPS receiver in the laptop bag and since it's got an integrated LTE modem with a 4G-enabled SIM, it sends location updates via SMS to a central server that I can access via the iPhone and view against a digital map."

Sunny blinked. "I'm not very technical. What's that in English?"

"Sam, break it down as if you were explaining to a five-year-old," Arun said from the front passenger seat.

"I know what 'patronise' means," Sunny warned.

"All right," Sam said. "You know what GPS is – satellites in space to pinpoint a position on land?"

"Yeah, satnav."

"Well, the box I hid in the lining of the laptop bag sends its location to a database. I log in to that with my phone and it tells me where the receiver is at any time."

"It tells you where it is?"

"I just said that."

"Is that legal?"

"Sure. I got it off the internet. My dad saw this news story where this woman put a GPS chip into her son before he went off on a round-the-world trip so she could make sure he was safe. Dad said it'd be a good idea to put those into the vans at work since sometimes they get nicked when burglars try to steal the tools out of the back. He's a builder, you see. So I went online, found this website and bought some GPS trackers that we put in the vans. As soon as one got nicked, we knew where it was, sent the police round and it paid for itself. Luckily, I had a spare kicking around."

"And you gave this guy Thorne a bugged laptop just so you could use it to follow him?" Sunny shook her head. "Unbelievable."

Seeing that Sam was staring at her arm, Sunny looked down to see a claret-coloured stain appearing beneath the bandage. "Where are we now?" she asked.

"Just passing Farnborough on the left," Arun said.

"Donna, there's some services coming up. Let's pull over, have a comfort break, grab some food and try to work out what to do next."

"Can't you call for backup?" Donna said.

Sunny laughed. "And tell them what? That a bunch of schoolkids have trashed half of London and are now tracking kidnappers? Or that we're chasing a top-secret stolen weapon but they can't tell anyone? Sorry, but until we have something more solid, we're on our own."

16:15

"Man, what a dump," Donna said, dunking a limp fry in ketchup before popping it into her mouth and taking in the gloomy interior of the service station.

"I don't care what it looks like. I'm starving," Sam said, wrapping his mouth round his second burger.

Arun checked his watch again. "School's finished. Mum will be worried sick by now," he said, poking at a rubbery chicken nugget. "We really should phone home."

"You're right," Sunny said, walking up to the table. "The last thing we need is more missing persons reports."

She sat down with her tray. She had her jacket on to cover the bandage she had just changed.

"Here, use my phone," she said, holding out her mobile between bites of her veggie burger. "They're tracing yours," she said to Donna.

Sam took the phone and shrugged. "My parents are both out," he said.

"Then leave them a message," Sunny said. "Just don't tell them where you are."

Sam dialled and waited for the answerphone. "Hi, Mum," he said, after the bleep. "I'm, uh, staying over at Arun's after school. We've got science homework to do, um, building a robot, you know. Uh, cheers."

"You're not a very good liar," Donna said, sucking down the last of her cola.

Sam thought about saying something but decided against it.

Arun took the phone. The idea of his mother sitting alone, waiting for him to come home, caused an uncomfortable feeling inside his chest. He knew that she would be worried sick about what might have happened to both him and his father, knew that she would have needed someone close to hold on to, knew that he should be there with her instead of stuck in a grotty service station on a wild goose chase.

"Whatever you say, go easy," Sunny said gently. "Remember, they'll be listening in."

Arun wiped his eyes and keyed in the number.

Back in the Lal house, several agents jumped when the phone rang. Heidi, who had been collecting teacups, snatched the cordless phone from its stand.

"Hello? Lal residence," she said.

"Mum? It's me."

Relief surged through Heidi in a wave, washing her strength away and leaving her weak. She slumped on to a chair.

"Arun? Oh my gosh, where are you? How are you? What have you been doing? Who's wi—"

"Mum, I'm fine. Really, I'm fine. I'm with Sam and this girl Donna."

"You're what? I – I don't understand. Shouldn't you have—"

"Mum, it's OK. We decided to skip school and go to the cinema to hang out and stuff."

"You did what? What stuff? Arun, I am very disappoint—"

"Look, Mum, it'll have to wait. I'll be home later and you can tell me off then."

"Now, you listen to me, young man. I want you home—"

"Yeah, yeah. Just chill, Mum, OK?" He hung up.

Heidi stared at the phone and screamed.

One of Quinn's men stood frozen in the doorway, like a rabbit seeing a hawk swooping down. He smiled, shrugged and said, "Kids, eh?"

He ran before Heidi could throw the phone at his head.

* * *

Arun put the phone down on the sticky tabletop, his heart pounding.

"Wow," Sunny said. "She was cross. I heard that from here." She popped two painkillers into her mouth and washed them down with a gulp of water.

Arun crossed his arms and glared at her. "I don't like lying to my mum," he said.

"OK, tell her the truth then." Sunny slid the phone back to him. "Tell MI6 where we are so they can come take us all in and try to save the day themselves. Then watch them mess it up and count how many people die."

Arun pushed the phone towards Donna. She stood up and scowled at it.

"I don't need to call anyone," she said.

"There's your mother—" Sunny started to say.

"Who won't be home until late," Donna said. "She's working on some big case and I won't see her for days, all right? You mummies' boys can call home and get tucked in at night. Good for you. Me, I take care of myself." She ran for the toilets before anyone could see her cry.

"Ouch," Sam said. "What brought that on?"

"Don't be too hard on her," Sunny said. "She's been through a lot."

"Like what?" Arun asked, curious.

Sunny sighed and leaned towards the centre of the table. "Promise me that what I'm about to tell you doesn't go beyond the three of us, you understand?"

The boys nodded.

"OK. Donna's parents met at Cambridge where they both studied law," she said.

Sam let out a low whistle. "Cool."

"When they left, they both joined a big City law firm. They were young and worked hard. Times were good and so was the money. Before long, Donna's dad started using illegal drugs – first speed, then cocaine."

"Not cool," Sam muttered.

"It started out as a thing he did to keep himself going, to work the long hours. Then it became a social thing at work. Donna's mum found out and hit the roof so he promised to quit." Sunny glanced towards the toilets. "Trouble is, he didn't. As time went on, he started stealing money from work to feed his habit."

Arun slowly shook his head. "That explains a lot."

"Angie, that's Donna's mum, finally had enough and turned him in to the police, complete with a watertight prosecution case for the CPS. He got five years."

"Yow," Sam said. "Harsh."

"Prison can be tough, especially if you're a City lawyer.

In order to survive in there, Donna's dad cut some deals, helped various gang bosses with their legal affairs and in return got looked after. When he came out, he had plenty of work waiting for him, and later moved into the supply side of the trade."

"He became a dealer?" Arun said, eyes wide.

"Yep. Donna's mum divorced him the first chance she got but he was still a good enough lawyer to get visitation rights, so every other weekend Donna gets to stay with dad and his lovely mates, which is presumably where she's learned all her handy skills. So try and be nice to her, OK? You might be the only real friends she's got."

At the Lal house Quinn's agent checked the message again to ensure he had not misread it, then dialled his boss.

"Gaffer," he said, when Quinn picked up. "Guess what? Mrs L just got a call from her missing boy."

"Really? What's he doing? Sniffing glue with his girlfriend?" Quinn said.

"Not quite. I ran a trace on the mobile and they're at Fleet Services, down on the M3."

"Fleet? What the heck is he doing there?"

"That's a question you should ask DC Patel. He was using her phone."

16:22

"They're moving again," Sam said, back in the Audi. "Heading south on Weston Road."

"That doesn't help me," Donna said. "Where do I come off the M3?"

"Junction 5. It's the next one. Exit and take the first left for the A287 south."

"Gotcha."

Sunny leaned over to look at the phone. "Can I see that?" she asked. Sam handed it to her and Sunny examined the screen for a few seconds. "Oh my gosh," she said. "I know where they're going."

"You do? Then maybe we can cut them off," Arun said. "Get there ahead of them and grab Dad before they can—"

"It won't be that simple," Sunny said. "We're going to need help."

"From who? You already said we're on our own."

She started tapping a number into her phone.

"Who's left to call?" Arun asked.

"We've run out of friends, so it's time to call an enemy."

She waited for the call to connect.

"Phil? It's Sunny... Yeah, I know... Yep... It's a long story... I know... Look, I need a favour... Yeah... Can you get me the number of a bloke over at MI6? Goes by the name of Quinn."

16:35

Two Special Escort Group police motorcycles had joined Quinn's pair of Range Rovers at Hammersmith, carving open a route through the early rush-hour traffic heading west. The convoy was now on the M25, passing Heathrow Airport on the left.

Green, sitting next to him in the back of the lead car, read from his phone. "They say the RAF Chinook was shot down by the Taliban in Helmand Province, killing all twenty Special Forces personnel on board," he said. "That was the official version."

"Except three of those dead soldiers show up today, alive and well – until three o'clock this afternoon, that is," Quinn said. "Have you run facial recognition, matching the rest of them against the crowd shots from Victoria?"

"We're working on it, but there's a lot of footage."

"Keep at it. Something will give."

"What are you thinking, gaffer?"

"I'm thinking our boy Thorne has had this planned for years, just waiting for the right time to make his move.

I reckon he helped these chaps fake their deaths so they could move around freely and he's had them on the payroll ever since."

Quinn's phone rang. He saw the caller ID, smiled and answered.

"Well, well, DC Patel. I was wondering when I'd be hearing from you."

"Quinn?" Sunny said.

"The one and only. What can I do you for?"

"I know where the MANDROID fleet is kept and I know that Thorne is almost there. He's going to steal it, Quinn."

Quinn sat bolt upright. "You know we can't let that happen."

"Tell me about it. It's a weapon, Quinn. In the wrong hands that thing could kill millions. You have to stop him."

"I'm on my way. Tell me what you know."

The minister answered his phone, holding up a hand for quiet in the CITADEL boardroom.

"It's my man at SIS," he said, lowering the handset. "Says Thorne is poised to attack MANDROID control."

"That's preposterous!" exclaimed Director Phelps "There's no way Galahad could penetrate that base."

"Didn't you say he was a near genius?" someone asked.

"Genius is one thing, suicidal is another."

"One question," the minister said, fixing his gaze on Phelps. "Is it at Lasham?"

The colour drained from Phelps's face and his head fell into his hands.

"I'll take that as a yes. How would my man know that unless he was on the right track?" He put the phone to his mouth once more. "Quinn? I'm going to put you on speakerphone. You'll be talking to Brian Phelps, Project Director. He can answer your questions."

The minister placed the phone in the middle of the table.

"Phelps? I don't have much time," Quinn said through the handset. "My contact tells me this thing is kept at Lasham Airfield. Is that true? If so, then I need to know everything about the facility, specifically its security. How long will it take Thorne to reach the weapon, assuming he's able to get in?"

Phelps stood and took one of the A1 sheets of paper on the table. He picked up a marker and began sketching a diagram.

"Hello? Are you still there?" Quinn said.

"Yes, just a minute," Phelps said, finishing a crude drawing and getting his thoughts in order. "I'll send you a photo of this. All right. Lasham was built and used by the

RAF during the Second World War. The MOD later sold it to a gliding club, but kept ownership of a pocket of the airfield on the eastern side. When we were looking for a base of operations, Lasham was selected because of its proximity to London and quiet location."

"So everyone thinks it's a civilian airfield?" Quinn said.

"Yes," answered Phelps. "For that reason we built the MANDROID test lab and hangar underground, which makes it impossible to attack. The whole facility is completely hidden. There are one hundred Royal Marines permanently stationed there and, since there are so few entry points, it's easy to defend. There's no way that Galahad or anyone else can get in."

"That's where you're mistaken," Quinn said.

"What do you mean?" Phelps countered. "We've run through every scenario. It's impregnable."

"All I'm saying is that an underground base needs external access. Food has to come in, waste has to go out, you've got plumbing, you've got power. A rat can squeeze in through the smallest crack. So, too, can these rats."

"What are you saying, Quinn? Can you see a weakness?" General McAllister said.

"No, just that if there is one, you can bet your backside that these guys will find it."

"I see," McAllister said. "Director Phelps, can you patch me through on a secure line? I think our men in MANDROID base could use a heads-up."

"Here you are, General," Clements said, handing a phone to McAllister. "We're going to connect you to MANDROID control. There'll be a Captain Whitby on the line..."

Quinn ended the call.

"Looks like Patel was right," he said to Green sitting next to him in the Range Rover. "We're going to need backup. Call base and tell them to send everything they've got, kitchen sink and all. We have to stop Thorne."

"Right away, gaffer."

In the Lal family's living room, the agent put down his phone and began to disassemble the call-monitoring equipment.

Heidi, perched on the sofa, was watching him. "Is that it?" she asked. "You're going home already?"

A second agent came in, a biscuit in his hand.

"Call came through from the boss," the first agent said to him. "Time to pack up."

The newcomer glanced at his watch. "Cutting it close," he said, and began to help clear the equipment away.

"Keep going on Alton Road," Sam said to Donna, as she drove the Audi down the country lane. "We're almost there."

Sunny winced and saw blood staining the bandage again. She quickly covered her arm with her jacket before any of the children could see.

Thorne's SUV pulled up beside a chain-link fence on the far side of Lasham Airfield.

"Sir, everything's set and ready to go," Lewis said, holding his phone to his chest. "Explosives are set at all three substations. Just awaiting your command."

"Excellent," Thorne said. "Commence Phase Four."

"Hit it," Lewis said into the phone.

16:42

Crouching down behind a white energy-company van, a man in white overalls pressed the detonator button on the box in his hand.

There was a soft *CRUMP* sound and a ball of fire ripped through the electricity substation, blasting the grey transformers into twisted strips of metal and shattering the ceramic insulators. The shockwave from the explosion smashed the compound's wooden fencing to splinters and rocked the van.

In the underground MANDROID Command Bunker, every light and computer screen died, plunging the room into blackness.

Whitby, who was holding the phone, managed to say "What the heck?" before red emergency lights flickered on and computer systems bleeped back into life.

"Captain Whitby, what's happening?" McAllister's voice buzzed from the phone, but Whitby wasn't listening.

"Burge, what's going on?" Whitby demanded. "I thought

we had redundancy built in?"

"We do, sir. We're on generator power right now, but we shouldn't be. We have three separate power supplies coming in, so if we lose one, another should kick in."

"But it didn't. Why not?"

"Sir, the only way that would've happened is if all three supplies … went down at the same time." He stopped, a look of growing horror on his face.

"Hello? Hello? Whitby, what's happening there?" McAllister said, shouting into the phone from the CITADEL boardroom.

"What's going on?" a minister said, rising to his feet.

"The attack has begun," McAllister said, looking directly at Phelps. "We're about to find out if this base of yours really is as secure as you think it is."

"I need all cameras back online now!" Whitby roared, as Marines ran from desk to desk, checking systems and rerouting the emergency power.

"Sir, all perimeter cameras are working again, except for 13-C," an operator said. "It's the only one that's stayed offline."

* * *

Inside a small wooden hut on the surface of the airfield, the electrical flex to Camera 13-C hung limply and one of Thorne's units was busy lifting the floor to expose a concrete-lined hole in the ground.

One of the squad tied a rope to a metal eye on the casing of a copper cylinder, that was partially sheathed in a concrete jacket with a metal box attached at one end.

"Easy now," the team leader said, and the troops strained to lower the metre-long device into the open ventilation shaft. "Whatever you do, don't drop it."

"Pull up the schematics for Shed 13-C," Whitby said, crouching down beside the monitor.

"Yes, sir." The Marine's fingers danced over the keyboard and a CAD drawing appeared, showing a side elevation of the underground complex.

"Zoom in."

The operator dragged the cursor to show a close-up of Sector 13-C.

"What's that?" Whitby said, drawing his finger down a pair of vertical lines.

"Ventilation shaft, sir. Feeds air into the cooling system for the main servers."

"Is there any way a man could get down there?"

"No, sir. It's a hundred-metre drop, with fans here, here and here."

Whitby breathed a sigh of relief. "So why would anyone be interested in it? Burge, where are my radio comms?"

"You don't need the radio," Burgess said, holding up the secure phone. "The general's still on hold."

The heavy device was now suspended fifty metres inside the shaft, hanging from a nylon rope tied to a wooden beam inside the shed.

Outside, the four men were running as fast as they could towards the fence.

Sitting in the SUV, his eyes fixed on the second hand of his watch, Thorne counted, "Three ... two ... one ... boom!"

16:54

Inside the ventilation shaft the suspended device exploded, its shockwave muffled in the tunnel.

All the lights and computers went dead again in the Command Bunker, accompanied by an acrid smell of ozone and burning plastic. This time the power did not come back on.

"What's going on?" Captain Whitby demanded, red phone in hand. "I thought we were on generator power."

"Sir, we are," a Marine said, his voice sounding small in the dark.

"So where's the power?"

Whitby pulled up his sleeve to check his watch. The second hand had stopped.

"Sir, torches don't work," a voice said.

Whitby could hear the *click-click* of someone trying a switch again and again. He put the phone to his ear but it was completely dead.

A cigarette lighter sparked into life and Burgess held up

the tiny flame.

"Sir," he said, "without lights and power, we're as good as dead."

McAllister stared at the phone in his hand.

"General, is something wrong?" a minister said.

"Yes. Most definitely," the general replied. "Director Phelps, this is a secure landline, yes?"

"That's right," Phelps said. "The cable goes direct from here to MANDROID Control. Why?"

"Because the line just went dead – and I mean completely dead. No hiss, no crackle."

"It's too deep to be cut," Phelps said. "That's impossible."

McAllister sighed. "I've been hearing that word a lot this afternoon."

Phelps stared into space for a moment. "Unless..." he started to say.

There was a tap on the door and Clements bounded in.

"Sir, we've just lost all contact with MANDROID Control," he said. "No comms, no telemetry, no alarms – nothing. All their systems are down. Every last one of them."

Sitting in the black SUV, Thorne pressed the talk button on his walkie-talkie. "All teams, converge on the main entrance. Phase Five ready to commence."

Down in the Command Bunker, candle wax dribbled down the face of a monitor. Worried faces bobbed in the circle of light as Whitby addressed his troops.

"—a hundred men who we can't mobilise without working comms. We have no radio, no intercom, no mobiles – we might as well use carrier pigeon."

"Sir, night scopes are useless. Goggles too," Burgess reported.

"Right. It looks like we're going to have to fight in the dark. Make your way to the other Marines, have them ready their weapons and take up defensive positions in the corridors. The loading bay will have to be the main point of defence."

"Permission to speak freely, sir," Burgess said.

Whitby looked at his junior officer and nodded. "Permission granted."

"Sir ... Ian ... this is suicide. We can't fight an enemy we can't see. If we shoot blind, we might end up killing each other."

"Burge, you know we can't surrender this facility."

"Sir, if we don't, we're all going to die."

* * *

"There it is!" Arun shouted, bolting upright in the front seat. "There's the airfield."

Donna slowed the car as it neared the expanse of green field and grey concrete. "Where next?" she said.

"Follow the perimeter road east … towards the end of the main runway," Sam said, squinting at his phone. "Then … oh. It looks like a field."

"A field? Let me see that," Sunny said, taking the phone. "Why would Thorne be standing in a field? Do you think he found your little tracking toy and chucked it out the window?"

Sam shrugged, but Arun's mind was working furiously.

"Sam, how close up can you see on the map?" he asked.

"Up to twenty square metres. I can see cars and bushes."

"That's good enough," Arun said.

"Good enough for what?" Sunny said.

"You'll see."

A line of vehicles drove along the track towards a large barn at the edge of Lasham Airfield, kicking up a cloud of dust. As they drew closer, the black Jeep Cherokee in front accelerated towards the barn doors.

With a crash the wood splintered as the Jeep smashed through. Machine-gun fire punctuated the afternoon air, followed by muffled explosions, then silence. A man wearing a gas mask came out and held a thumb aloft.

The cars and vans pulled up outside and twenty-five mercenaries got out. They stopped to check their packs, putting down their guns to adjust Kevlar vests and tighten up grenade belts.

Thorne stopped to admire his small army and allowed himself another smile. Then he snapped his fingers and Krishan and Moss were dragged from the white transit van and hauled before him, their hands and legs still bound. A soldier whipped off the hoods and they lowered their heads, blinking in the daylight.

"Krishan, Double-X, here's what you need to know: in a few minutes I will have full control of the MANDROID prototype. It will be leaving with me. I will ask you for the password to the laptop containing the encrypted access codes. You will tell me and die quickly, or you will refuse and die slowly. It doesn't trouble me either way. When I am far from here with my prize, I will be able to hack in to all MANDROID systems at my leisure, so it doesn't really make a difference. You can decide how smart you want to be on the way down."

The men gathered up their weapons and the group marched into the barn.

"Director Phelps, I have a hundred men cut off from the outside world and a weapon about to be stolen. What's happening over there?" McAllister said in the CITADEL boardroom, dabbing his brow with a handkerchief.

Phelps removed his glasses and rubbed his eyes. "Let me think..." he said. "The phone died, even though it's a secure line. At the exact same moment we lost all telemetry. *Our* systems are working, but theirs are all down ... which would imply a localised loss of all electronic..." He cursed, his face draining of colour. "I know what Galahad's done, and if I'm right, there's nothing that can stop him."

Inside the barn, Thorne stepped over the unconscious body of a soldier in civilian clothing, walked up to a wooden beam and opened a hidden flap. Inside was a fingerprint scanner. He pressed his thumb against it and a grinding sound came from beneath the wooden floor.

"Move away from the centre," he said.

His team stepped back; then, with a hydraulic whine, a section of floor slowly dropped down and slid aside, exposing a square metal platform five metres wide.

"Teams Two, Three, Eleven and Twelve, secure the dock," Thorne commanded.

Twelve soldiers went to the platform, including two carrying a six-barrelled GE M134 Minigun and two hauling a large pack full of car batteries to power it. An electrical cable led from the pack to the tripod-mounted gun and an ammunition belt fed into it from another backpack. The men all pulled on night-vision goggles and gas masks, making them resemble giant insects.

"Ready?" Thorne asked.

His answer was the clatter of rounds being chambered and magazines snapped into position as the twelve men locked and loaded their weapons.

"Ready," one of them said.

Thorne pressed a button on the panel and the platform of mercenaries began to descend.

Having taken up a defensive position in the MANDROID loading bay, Burgess snapped a glow stick, shook it and tossed it overarm. It bounced and landed in the middle of a large open area; its dim light barely reached the concrete walls.

"Listen, what's that?" Burgess said, as the sound of hydraulics reached him.

"The service lift," Whitby said, crouching behind a wooden crate. He readied his assault rifle. "Someone's coming. Everyone, get ready!"

The sixty Marines guarding the dock took aim in the direction of the lowering platform.

17:01

"According to the GPS, the laptop's over there, in that barn," Sam said, shielding his eyes as he looked across the field towards the building with numerous cars parked outside.

Sunny leaned against her Audi, idling by the perimeter road, and tried to ignore the dull ache in her left arm. "That's almost a mile away, across an open field. Good luck trying to sneak up on it."

Donna scowled at her, then said, "Arun, you said you had an idea, back in the car."

He nodded. "Sam, can I see the map?"

Sam handed him the iPhone. Arun looked at the screen and smiled. "I thought so," he said.

"What is it now?" Sunny said.

"Here, take a look," Arun said, offering her the phone.

She looked at it and shrugged. "It's a satellite picture of the field we're looking at. What about it?"

"Look again," Arun said. "Where's the barn?"

"Huh?" Sunny looked again, moved the picture around

and tried zooming out and in again. "It's not there," she said finally.

"Right, which means it's been removed from the photo—"

"Which you'd only do if you wanted to hide it," Donna said, and grinned.

"All we have to do now is see if any other buildings have been removed from the map and see if we can peek inside one of them."

Sunny nodded. "How about that one over there?" She pointed to a low hut, some 200 metres away.

They began walking.

As they approached Junction 5 of the M3, the two police motorcyclists waved farewell and pulled into the middle lane, allowing the two Range Rovers to zoom past.

Quinn, sitting inside the second vehicle, whipped round to watch the motorcycles disappear into the distance.

"Where the blooming heck are they going?" he said. "We're almost there and we need everyone we've got for this!"

"They've been told to stand down," Green said.

"They've been told to what?" Quinn exploded. "By who?"

"By me," Green said, pressing the barrel of his Browning into Quinn's ribs. He reached into the older man's jacket and removed his gun.

Brown, sitting in the front passenger seat, turned, his pistol also trained on Quinn. "Sorry, gaffer," he said. "It's nothing personal. Just Thorne made us a better offer."

Quinn was apoplectic. "Don't tell me you're all in on this?" he thundered. "No! I made you! I hand-picked this team! Trained you all!"

"But you're not paying us five million pounds each," Brown said. "Don't worry, you'll get your chance. The boss wants a word and then you can fix your own price."

"It has to be locked," Sam said.

They had reached the hut, which stood tall and narrow like an outside toilet.

"How do you know?" Donna said, approaching the door. She looked for a lock, couldn't see one and pushed. The door swung open.

"Must be my magic touch," she said, going inside.

Sam followed her in, then stopped to inspect the inside of the door.

"Look," he said, pointing at a metal plate. "I was right. It's a solenoid lock, magnetically controlled. You'd need a special card to get in here."

"Except we didn't," Sunny said. "Which means what?"

"The lock isn't working?" Sam said.

The four of them squeezed into the tiny hut.

"What are we looking for?" Arun asked.

"I dunno, anything that looks wrong, I suppose," Sunny said.

"You mean like carpet?" Donna said, toeing the green Astroturf that lined the floor of the hut.

Together, the four of them worked to get a grip on the edge of the plastic grass and lifted it up. A wooden trapdoor lay beneath, set into the planks of the floor.

"Bet it's locked," Sam said.

Donna took the pocket knife from Arun, opened a blade and inserted it into the crack between the hatch and the floor. She pressed gently downwards on the blade.

"Careful! You'll break it," Sam said.

The trapdoor lifted slightly. Quickly, everyone dug their fingers into the gap and soon they had the hatch leaning against the wall. Underneath, a tunnel led downwards, with rungs set into the concrete side.

"That should have been locked too," Sam said, tapping a metal plate on the underside of the hatch. "Something's wrong here."

"What's the plan now?" Sunny asked.

"This tunnel leads down," Arun said. "So the MANDROID

base must be underground. If we can get there before Galahad, maybe we can stop him."

"How?" Sunny said.

"I don't know, but we can't let him steal it. If Galahad's turned it into a weapon, then a lot of people could get hurt because of my dad's work. I can't let that happen. Besides, if we can stop him, maybe he'll let Dad go."

"You're dreaming," Sunny said. "You've seen the kind of thugs we're up against: ex-army nutcases packing serious firepower. There's no way I'm letting a bunch of schoolkids go anywhere near that."

"There's something else you should know," Sam said. "There's a bomb involved. A nuclear bomb."

"I don't believe you," Sunny said, her voice ragged.

"It's true," Donna said. "There's a bomb loaded up and ready. It told us."

"So what part of 'nuclear bomb' did I not hear properly?" Sunny said. "There is no way I'm letting you kids go down there. We wait for help."

"I don't think you have a lot of choice in this," Arun said, locking eyes with Sunny. "Let's say one of us decided to try and hold you back while the other two started climbing down the ladder – you wouldn't be able to stop us, not with that arm." Arun's voice was low and steady. "But that would be silly; we're on the same side and we want the same thing, to get our loved ones back."

Sunny bit her lower lip and nodded. "I'm hearing you."

"You know I have to go down there," Arun said. "If there's any chance I can stop Galahad and help my dad, then I have to try. You'd do the same."

"We're losing time talking about this," Donna said. She brought her face close up to Sunny's. "Look at me. Do you have any doubt that I will kick you in that busted arm of yours as many times as it takes for you to see sense?"

"All right, all right," Sunny said. "I'll make you a deal. Quinn's on the way with backup and they'll need to know what's going on. If you go down there, promise me you'll come back up as soon as you know what's happening, you hear? Or at the first sign of any danger. Promise?"

"You're not coming with us?" Sam asked.

Sunny shook her head. "I can't. My arm's knackered. I can hardly lift it, let alone climb down that ladder."

"Good. We need someone to stay up here and keep guard," Donna said.

"OK, that's settled then," Arun said, lowering himself into the tunnel.

"Wait!" Sunny said. "You'll need this." She delved into her handbag and held out a slim Maglite torch.

"Thanks," Arun said.

"Oh, I forgot all about this," Sunny said, pulling out the walkie-talkie she had taken from the wrecked ambulance. She switched it on and they heard the crackle of static. "Still works," she said, handing it to Arun.

"What else you got in there?" Donna asked, eyeing the bag.

Sunny took out the Browning pistol and checked the clip. "Don't get any ideas," she said to Donna. "It's bad enough me letting you kids go down there. I am not giving you a gun."

"Ohhh." Donna's smile faded and she turned to follow Arun into the tunnel.

"Remember, get back up here at the first sign of trouble," Sunny said, watching the children disappear into the hole. "And, please, be careful."

"Phelps, I didn't understand a single word you just said," snapped the minister.

"Could you please run through that once more?" another official said.

Phelps stopped pacing the boardroom and scratched his chin. "Galahad must have detonated an EMP. EMP – electromagnetic pulse – is something we've known about for years—"

"Yes, we all got that, but I thought it only came from a nuclear explosion," McAllister said.

"Oh, no," Phelps said. "You can make a pulse bomb if you know how. As I said, you wrap a copper wire tightly round a tube packed with explosives, charge the wire with a generator to create an intense magnetic field and then blow the core, sending out an electromagnetic shockwave. That's what I was trying to—"

"And this would destroy all electronic devices in range?"

"Absolutely. It'd be like a hundred lightning bolts hitting at the same time, only without the electricity."

There was silence for a full minute.

Finally McAllister said, "But what about this MANDROID device? Won't it be destroyed too, by this EMP?"

Phelps shook his head. "No, the lab housing it is a giant Faraday cage; the mesh blocks electromagnetic radiation. Plus, it has its own protection."

"So you mean to say I have men stuck down there in the dark, with no equipment to help them, while Thorne just walks in and steals the thing?" McAllister slumped back. "Good heavens."

"Phelps, is there anything we can do?" the minister said.

"Yes, we can pray for a miracle."

* * *

The concrete walls slid silently upwards as the lift platform descended. Six of Thorne's team, perched at the front, unclipped grenades from their belts and pulled the pins, holding down the safety levers.

"How come the lift's still working?" Captain Whitby said, keeping his weapon aimed at the hydraulic column that supported the platform.

"All the lift controls and machinery's on top," Burgess said. "Whatever's happened must only be affecting systems down here."

"As soon as you get a clear shot, men, open fire!" Whitby called out, his voice echoing. "Hit them with everything you've got."

"Sir, the lift!" someone shouted as a square slab of steel appeared in the ceiling. A small gap opened between the metal base of the platform and the concrete roof, followed by the clang of metal cylinders bouncing off the stone floor.

"What the—"

The stun grenades exploded with searing flashes of blinding light, obliterating the little vision that the Royal Marines had. Ground-shaking, teeth-rattling shock blasts followed, their volume magnified by the enclosed space.

Whitby couldn't hear himself scream; momentarily blinded and deafened, all he knew was the force of the explosions reverberating through his body, like someone standing next to a giant bass speaker at a heavy metal concert. White smoke filled the dock and the Marines nearest to it started to collapse one after the other.

"Gas!" Whitby yelled. "Fall back!" He pressed his sleeve over his nose and mouth.

The six men at the front of the descending platform stood aside, clearing a path for the six-barrelled electric minigun. The gunner lined up the stricken Marines through his night-vision goggles and opened fire, sending bullets churning through the air at a rate of twenty rounds per second.

Instantly the packing crates that the Marines had been using for cover were blasted into matchwood.

Whitby thought he was yelling, "Fall back! Fall back!" but he couldn't tell. He turned and ran, stumbling his way along the wall towards where he thought the door was.

The six spinning gun barrels slowed and the whine of the motor died as the gunner released the trigger. He looked around the empty dock and smiled.

17:08

"This is a very bad idea," Sam said, looking up at the tiny circle of light far above. His voice echoed in the long tunnel.

"Shhh!" Donna hissed. "Listen."

The children stopped climbing and clung to the cold metal rungs, straining to hear. From below came the muffled thump of explosions and the chatter of automatic gunfire.

"Sounds like a war zone down there," Arun said.

"That's a sign of danger," Sam said, his voice shaking. "Can we go back up now?"

Arun peered down, took a penny from his trouser pocket and dropped it, counting the seconds until he heard it land with a soft clink.

"We're almost there," Arun said. "Think about it, Sam. We're past the point of no return; it'd take you longer to climb back up than to carry on to the bottom."

"I don't mind."

"We're just going for a quick look," Donna said.

Sam sighed and started climbing down again.

"The dock is secure," squawked a voice so loudly and suddenly that Arun jumped and almost slipped. He grabbed the walkie-talkie from his pocket and pressed it against his chest to muffle the speaker.

"Excellent," said Thorne's voice. "Commence sweep-up operations."

"Will do. We're sending the lift back up. Come down whenever you're ready."

Arun stared at the radio. "They're here!" he said. "We have to hurry!"

"Fifteen minutes until the transport arrives," Lewis reported to Thorne while they waited in the barn for the lift to return.

The door to the barn swung open and Quinn came in, prodded at gunpoint by his former colleagues.

Thorne was unable to hide his delight. "Special Agent Quinn! What a pleasure it is to finally meet you. I've heard so much about you."

"Don't believe any of it," Quinn growled, "especially if it came from my missus."

Thorne shot his cuffs and adjusted his tie. "I suppose you worked out enough to become a threat, which is why my men brought you here."

"Your men?" Quinn said. "They were my men before you bought them off."

Thorne smiled. "You know, Quinn, the sad part was how easy it was. They couldn't wait to be rid of you, always barking at them, pushing them around."

Quinn glared at his men; none met his gaze.

"You're a dinosaur, Quinn," Thorne continued, "a relic from a bygone age. You're a bully, who's rude, arrogant, self-centred—"

"Those are my good points," Quinn said. "Can you stop blathering and get on with it?"

"Here's the deal," Thorne said. "Ten million pounds to come and work for me. Tell me everything you know about the inner workings of His Majesty's secret service. Otherwise..." He drew a finger across his throat.

"You really think I'd betray my country for a toe-rag like you?" Quinn said. "Dream on. If all I cared about was money, I wouldn't be doing this. Some things are more important."

"I told you," Saipher said. "We should kill him now."

"No," Thorne said. "He's worth more to us alive than dead."

Saipher snorted. "Let me know the second that changes."

There was a ping as the lift arrived.

"Let's go," Thorne said. "Mr Quinn can watch while I take back what's mine."

Arun switched on the Maglite, illuminating the concrete corridor. He saw a white sign with red letters: "4-F".

Donna and Sam stepped down from the ladder.

"Now what?" Sam whispered, shivering from the cold.

"Check it," Donna said, pointing at a white square on the wall.

They crept closer. Arun shone the torch and lit up a laminated map of the facility.

"It's a fire plan," he whispered, "showing exits and meeting points."

"Does it tell us where we are?" Sam asked.

"Maybe... Looks like 4-F is part of a corridor running all the way round a central hangar. We're here, on the west side," Arun said, pointing.

"Someone's coming!" Donna said, her sharp ears picking up the sound of approaching boots. "Quick! There's a door this way."

She pushed and it swung open. The three children dived into the blackness beyond as a small group of armed Marines felt their way past in the dark.

17:14

"Where are we?" Donna whispered.

Arun swept the torch beam in a wide arc. "We're in the hangar at the centre of the base," he said, unable to see any walls to the front or sides.

"This place is huge," Sam said. "I can't even see the ceiling."

"I saw something – over there." Donna pointed. "It was shiny."

Arun stepped forward into the black void. "Stay close," he said, inching his way towards a massive glittering object in the middle of the hangar.

"It looks like ... a camper van?" Arun said, playing the torch beam across the gleaming blue and gold surfaces. "What's that doing down here?"

Sam watched closely, counting off twelve thick wheels and noting the curved cockpit-style windscreen. "Arun, it's more like a truck," he said. "I'm not sure what kind, but it's definitely a vehicle."

Donna slapped the back of his head. "Like, duh! It's the

thing – can't you see? Every tank, plane, bus, whatever that was in the laptop had the same blue and gold colours, same as our school, same as this."

Arun's mouth fell open. "Donna's right," he said. "This must be part of the MANDROID fleet."

"Where's the rest of it?" Donna asked, looking around. "There were planes and trucks."

Another explosion tore through the corridor outside, nearer this time, followed by more machine-gun fire.

"I don't know about you, but I'd rather be in there than out here." Donna walked up to the vehicle and climbed a small ladder set behind the front window bay. "Thought so," she said. "Here's a door. And before you say anything, Sam, it's already open. Bye." She climbed inside.

Sam and Arun looked at each other for a moment, then raced after her.

Arun ducked through the door of the vehicle into a small passageway, shielding his eyes from the bright lights that had switched themselves on. Donna was looking around, her eyes wide.

"Oh. My. Days," she said quietly.

Arun joined her and saw that a central passageway ran the length of the vehicle. The floor was uneven and divided into sections of varying heights. Towards the front was a cockpit-style cabin with a vast array of instrument panels, switches, lights, levers, buttons, screens, dials, gauges and displays arranged in a horseshoe pattern round a single chair.

Another seat sat in the middle of the passage, halfway down the vehicle, with a bank of instruments on either side. Arun could make out a third chair positioned at the rear of the vehicle, also with an impressive instrument panel.

Sam squeezed in beside Arun and let out a low whistle.

"What do you make of it, Sam?" Arun asked.

"I've never seen anything like this before," Sam said. "I've seen pictures of the inside of the Space Shuttle but it's nothing compared to this."

"You're saying there's more stuff in here than in a spaceship?" Donna said.

Sam nodded and swallowed hard. "Yeah. Look at it! Some of these displays would suit an aircraft, others look more like they belong in a submarine. I can't make head nor tail of this."

Just then the door slammed shut.

Please identify yourselves.

The children jumped and Sam let out a small scream. The voice was coming from all around.

Goosebumps crawled over Arun's skin as a holographic display lit up on the inside of the front windscreen. He recognised it immediately as a diagram of the vehicle they were standing in. Three red lights glowed, showing the children's positions. Circles appeared around the red spots – circles with cross hairs.

"Who – who are you?" Arun stammered.

Please identify yourselves. You have ten seconds to comply before security countermeasures begin.

"It's the AI!" Sam said.

"Uh, my name is Arun Lal," Arun said, holding out his hands to show they were empty. "I'm not my dad, just so you know."

"Sam Evans," Sam said. "Please don't hurt us – we didn't mean to trespass or any—"

"Shhh! You're wasting time," Donna hissed, cuffing him. "I'm Donna Critchlow," she said in a firm voice. "Who wants to know?"

There was a bleep and dozens of red lights lit up around the cabin.

Commencing biometric scans. Please remain where you are.

"I don't like this!" Donna's voice started to rise in panic.

"Stay still, like it said," Arun commanded. "If it was going to harm us, it wouldn't have warned us first."

Scanning lasers blinked on and the cabin air turned pink as multiple grid lines of ruby light swept across the floor to the children's feet, then slowly worked their way upwards over ankles and shins.

Arun half expected to feel something, maybe some kind of tingling, but he reminded himself it was only light.

The beams swept upwards and Arun could see three-dimensional models appearing on the screen of himself, Donna and Sam.

When the lasers had scanned the last hairs on his head, they blinked off and the normal lighting returned.

Biometric scans complete. Please enter access codes.

"Access codes?" Sam was frozen, unable to think.

"Oh, for..." Donna pulled the Iron Man backpack from Sam's shoulders and plonked it down on the floor. She yanked out the portable hard drive and carried it to the front panel. "How do you wanna do this?" she said. "I don't see any USB slots."

A panel slid open revealing an array of docking ports.

Arun grabbed the lead from the pack and plugged one end into the hard drive and the other into the panel. "Ready," he said. "You can commence upload."

After a second, there was a soft bleep. *Access codes*

confirmed. All systems fully operational and now online. Welcome aboard, Commander Lal.

Donna laughed out loud. "Commander Lal? That's a good one!"

Arun ignored her. "Please identify yourself," he said to the computer voice.

I am MANDROID.

Outside, an explosion ripped through one of the hangar doors, blasting it inwards. Gunfire rattled and twenty Royal Marines sprinted into the dark room, returning fire as they ran.

"Sir! We're too late! The lights are on! Someone's already inside!" Burgess shouted to Whitby as he flung himself towards the huge vehicle in the middle of the space. Its interior cabin was illuminated and spotlights cast a warming glow around it, like a protective circle.

"We can use it as cover!" Whitby said. "If they don't want it damaged, they might not shoot if we're under it!"

A second explosion tore through the far door and the sound of running boots followed.

"At least ten of them," Whitby said, reaching the vehicle and looking through a pair of night-vision goggles he had salvaged from a fallen enemy soldier. "And they've got

237

rocket-propelled grenades! Take cover!"

Thorne's men sauntered across the open space, the lights from the vehicle framing them in silhouette and throwing long menacing shadows on the ground. They fanned out in a wide arc, weapons at the ready and closed in on the huddled Marines, ready for the kill.

17:23

Lewis pushed open the door to the MANDROID Command Bunker and led the way inside, sweeping the room with a powerful torch.

Thorne breezed in and set the laptop bag down on the nearest console. He opened it and removed the computer.

Saipher shoved Quinn forward, his wrists zip-tied tightly together behind him. "Stay outside and guard the door," Saipher hissed at Quinn's agents.

Two of Thorne's soldiers half carried, half dragged Krishan and Moss into the room. Another brought up the rear, machine gun in hand.

"Time's up," Thorne said, eyeing Moss and Krishan, his face illuminated by the laptop screen. "I want the password and access codes now."

"I don't know any password," Moss said.

"Galahad, your friend in the mask knows I won't talk," Krishan added.

Thorne sighed in an exaggerated world-weary manner. "I was hoping you'd say that. It makes this much easier.

Saipher, how much longer for your hack program to complete?"

"Five minutes max," Saipher said. "Then maybe another five to locate the access codes."

"Sir, the plane should be coming in about now," Lewis said.

"A plane?" Krishan repeated. "Oh, I see. It's your backup, in case you can't get MANDROID operational in time. Load it on a plane, fly it away and crack the security at your leisure."

Thorne smiled at Krishan. "You see? My plan is perfect. And all the time they kept saying that you were the genius, and treated me like ... your assistant. Well, maybe now I'll get the credit I deserve."

Quinn inched his way nearer to the huge picture window while Thorne was speaking.

"Any final words, Krishan? Any messages you want me to pass on to Heidi?"

Krishan glared at Thorne, his mouth tight with rage but he bit down, refusing to give him any satisfaction.

Thorne's smile vanished. "As you wish. You can kill them both now."

One of the mercenaries drew an automatic pistol and took aim at Krishan's head. His thumb flipped the safety catch and his index finger tightened on the trigger.

"Ahem," Quinn said loudly. "Before you do that, I think you should take a look out here." He nodded towards the window.

Thorne held up a finger for calm and darted to the window.

"No!" he said, eyes wide with astonishment.

"Looks like someone's beaten you to it," Quinn said, watching the scene unfolding below. "Remember when you said it couldn't work without the access codes? Looks like it's working fine to me."

Sitting by the top of the access tunnel, Sunny adjusted the bandage on her arm again. She rose to her feet as an overhead droning sound grew louder with each second.

She stepped out of the shed into the bright afternoon sunlight. Shielding her eyes with her hand, she looked up as a shadow roared past.

"What the—"

She stared upwards as a C-130 Hercules military transport plane rumbled in from the west and touched down with a screech of tyres on the airstrip runway.

"That's not supposed to be here," Sunny muttered over the roar of its propeller engines. She ran towards her car while the Hercules taxied towards the large barn.

"Hold fire until you get a clear shot," Whitby said to his remaining men, who were hunkered down behind the blue and gold vehicle for cover. "We can't afford to waste a single bullet."

The circle of Thorne's armed mercenaries tightened as they drew closer.

"Wait!" one of them shouted. He raised a fist and they stopped as one. The leader reached for his walkie-talkie and Thorne's voice crackled to life.

"—orders are to secure the MANDROID but, whatever you do, do not damage it," he said.

The man looked around in bafflement. "I'm sorry to have to break the news to you, boss, but these wee chappies we're facing have guns and they're cornered and they're hidin' behind the thing. What do you think is goin' to happen?"

"Listen to me, you idiot! Someone has got inside the vehicle. If you start shooting, its automated defence systems will—"

"Ah, put a sock in it, will ya? It's probably just some wee tech gadgie who's peein' his pants inside. You yourself said no one can operate it. If any of these fish heads shoots at me or my men, we shoot back. End of story." He killed the radio, cutting off Thorne's protests. "All right, boys," he said, "let's finish this."

"What's going on out there?" Donna said to herself, looking out of the window.

Proximity sensors detect armed intruders within the hangar area, replied MANDROID.

Sam and Arun pressed their faces to the window to get a better look.

"I can't see anything," Arun said. "Are those guys moving around in the dark?"

That is correct. The unidentified intruders are wearing visual-enhancement apparatus for low-light environments.

"Night-vision goggles?" Sam said.

"What else have they got?" asked Donna.

The windscreen display changed to a rotating three-dimensional diagram of the hangar with wireframe drawings of the MANDROID vehicle, the Royal Marines sheltering behind it, and the circle of mercenaries closing in.

The intruders are equipped with body armour, assault rifles, automatic pistols, grenades, plastic explosives, combat knives and rocket-propelled grenade launchers.

"You're kidding," Donna said.

"MANDROID, what do the other guys have?" Arun asked, looking closely at the screen.

Captain Whitby's personn—

"Captain? Wait, you know him?"

Captain Ian Whitby is commanding officer of the Royal Marines force tasked with the defence of this—

"OK, I get it. What's he got?"

Captain Whitby's personnel are equipped with assault rifles.

Arun paused, waiting for the AI to continue. It didn't. "That's it?" he said. "That's all they've got? They're going to get massacred!"

That is correct.

"Can't we do anything? To help them?" Arun's voice was rising.

Of course. Shall I switch to defensive configuration?

Sam, Arun and Donna looked at each other and shrugged.

"Sure, whatever. Just do something!" Arun said.

The floor lurched and there was a hum of rising power.

You should sit down and fasten your seat belts.

"All right!" Donna shouted, jumping into the middle seat.

244

"Time to find out what this sucker can really do!" The foam of the seat moulded itself round her, while the seat belt snaked round her shoulders and waist, automatically locking itself.

"I just hope it's not too late," Arun muttered, climbing into the front seat.

Whitby wiped his clammy hands on his combat trousers and resumed his position, crouched down behind one of the vehicle's huge wheels. His assault rifle rested on the tyre and he watched through the night-vision goggles as Thorne's men raised their weapons, taking aim.

"Steady, boys!" Whitby said to his troops. "On my command..."

"Sir, we're just aiming at shadows," Burgess said.

"Then make sure you hit them."

The green-lit image in Whitby's goggles jumped and a streak of static scrolled down. A low electronic hum immediately followed, coming from the vehicle his men were hiding behind.

"What the—" said Burgess.

"I thought all electrics were down?" Whitby said, glaring suspiciously up at the underside of the truck.

Without warning the vehicle shuddered, lurched and

rose up silently around the Marines, floating upwards and separating into different loosely hinged sections. Whitby could only stare, craning his neck at what had once been the cockpit, which was now elevated twenty metres above the floor.

"What's happening?" Donna cried as her stomach lurched downwards.

All around her panels were shifting and the floor beneath her feet fell away, dropping to become an upright wall. Her seat rotated, keeping her in a forward-facing position and the consoles stayed within reach, but otherwise the central passage had now become a vertical shaft. Donna craned her neck upwards and saw Arun's feet dangling from his chair. Below, she saw Sam, his knuckles white, with his fingers digging into the armrest.

From the outside the large multi-wheeled truck had changed into something else entirely. Its wheels had folded inwards, slats had opened and closed, parts slid into new positions and the bulk of the vehicle had risen into the air, supported by the rear section so that it resembled a giant humanoid figure, with two long standing sections like legs, a solid midsection, two trailing arm-like columns, and the original cockpit sitting on top like a head.

Grid lines criss-crossed the on-screen display in front of Arun's seat, each intercept point lighting up when it stopped on a weapon held by the three-dimensional images of the soldiers outside.

All targets locked, said MANDROID. *Please confirm if a lethal or non-lethal response is required.*

"Non-lethal," Arun said. "Don't kill anyone, right?"

Weapons systems armed. Guns released.

"Guns?" echoed Donna, from her seat below Arun. "This thing's got guns? Told you!"

"Hey, why do I get to be in its bum?" Sam protested from his position at the bottom of the central module.

Whitby stared as the two arm-like structures lifted with a hydraulic whine and levelled horizontally, seeming to reach out towards Thorne's men. Panels opened and automatic cannon slid into position.

BA-DA-BA-DA-BA-DA-BA-DA! A brief burst of deafening gunfire resounded and Whitby glanced away as the muzzle flashes flared inside his goggles.

When he looked up again, he heard the sound of men groaning. Thorne's soldiers were hopping around, either rubbing their stinging fingers and hands or holding shattered pieces of their firearms.

"Sir, what just happened?" Burgess whispered in awe.

"I think our new friend here just disarmed the bad guys," Whitby said, looking up at the MANDROID again. Wisps of smoke drifted from the gun barrels on its arms.

"Get the minigun in here now!" barked the enemy leader into his walkie-talkie. "And ready the RPGs!"

Thorne, watching from the Command Bunker, shouted into his radio. "No! Do not engage! You mustn't damage the prototype."

"Get real!" came the response. "You're not the one bein' shot at."

"Boss, more bad news for you," Saipher said, looking up from the laptop. "Someone's wiped all the MANDROID data from this PC, and that includes the access codes. It's empty."

Thorne's legs buckled and he fell into a chair. "No, no, no," he said. "This is not happening! My plan was perfect. I factored in every eventuality..."

"If I were you, I'd start working on a new plan – and fast," Saipher said.

Clements flung open the door to the CITADEL boardroom

and charged inside so fast that he tripped and almost slammed into the table.

"General McAllister, sir," he said breathlessly, "phone call for you from the MOD." He held out a cordless phone. "A police officer called from Lasham and said that a transport plane has landed to carry away the MANDROID prototype. She's going to try and stop it."

McAllister took the phone, listened carefully and nodded several times. "No, you did the right thing," he said. "It's not a hoax. I repeat, this is not a drill. How soon before we get troops there...? I see... All right, leave this with me. I have all the authorisation I need right here in this room."

He handed the phone back to Clements and stood up stiffly.

"Gentlemen, we have a major situation on our hands. Fortunately we also have a solution." He looked around at the tense faces of the men watching him. "We are all agreed, are we not, that we cannot, under any circumstances, allow this MANDROID device to fall into enemy hands?"

Everyone listening nodded.

"Very well. We have two RAF Typhoons on manoeuvres, fresh out of Coningsby. They're carrying live weapons and are fully equipped with Brimstone, Storm Shadow,

AMRAAM and ASRAAM missiles. Top speed is 1,500 miles per hour, which puts them no more than ten minutes from Lasham."

Phelps slammed his fist on the table. "No! You can't be serious. You can't destroy billions of pounds worth of research just like that."

"I think you'll find we can," snapped the minister. "General, what are the ... implications?"

McAllister hesitated. "Well ... worst case, we're talking about shooting down a fully fuelled aeroplane over a built-up area. There could be ... collateral damage. We will, of course, seek to avoid this at all costs."

"That's unacceptable. What's the alternative?"

"The alternative is that we allow this thing to be stolen and wake up one day to find it's dropped a nuclear bomb on London," said McAllister.

"I'll talk to the prime minister. I don't see that we have any choice in the matter."

The intruders have been disarmed with zero casualties, reported MANDROID.

Arun whooped, as much from relief as excitement. "All right!"

"I told you this thing was built to kick butt!" Donna

called up from her seat in the middle, a wide grin on her face.

"Not so fast," Sam called. His fingers were tapping a keyboard on the instrument panel before him and he was pressing other buttons.

"What's the matter?" Arun said.

"I'm not sure if I'm doing this right, but I think I've got an X-ray scan going of the external corridor and it looks like more bad guys are coming in with a really big gun."

Arun sat up. "MANDROID, is that correct?"

Affirmative. Hostile reinforcements are arriving now.

The remaining Marines stayed behind the towering figure of MANDROID for cover. Thorne's disarmed men had retreated into the shadows.

"What now, sir?" Burgess asked Whitby.

"We wait, either for them to come back or to get lost. Our job is to remain here, to guard this thing."

Burgess grinned. "I'm not sure who's guarding who, sir."

There was a clank of metal on concrete and muffled voices drifted across. Whitby turned his night-vision goggles in the direction of the sound and swore.

"What is it?" Burgess asked.

"The minigun. They brought it round the side."

"With us in the open? We've got to take cover."

"Too late for that, Burge."

The curtain of darkness was shredded by the lightning and thunder of twenty 7.62mm shells firing per second, aimed directly at MANDROID.

A moment later, five tank-busting rocket-propelled grenades streaked across the hangar from different directions, all zeroing in on the same target.

17:33

A storm of white-hot metal streaked across the darkened hangar and slammed into the midsection of MANDROID, sending it staggering back.

Donna screamed as the instrument panel in front of her exploded into a shower of sparks and a stream of heavy bullets hammered the wall in front of her.

Arun stared in horror at the screen before him as five arrows vectored in at high speed towards the on-screen image of MANDROID.

"Hold on!" he cried.

MANDROID's outstretched arms twitched and its automatic cannon fired five bursts. Bullets ripped into the rocket-propelled grenades, detonating them in mid-air, the orange fireballs throwing huge twisting shadows across the walls.

The slew of bullets from the minigun continued to blast away at the MANDROID's midsection, pounding at its armour and sending sparks flying. Chips of metal broke away and armour-piercing rounds ricocheted wildly around the hangar. Pushed off balance by the onslaught, one of its huge metal feet crashed down next to Burgess as it steadied itself.

But like a boxer bringing up his guard, MANDROID raised its left arm in a shielding movement and the stream of bullets ripped into it. Then its right arm swung round and took aim at the minigun. The cannon fired once and the minigun exploded, hurling the gunner into the air.

Whitby squinted through the smoke and wiped an arm across his forehead. "Thank you," he said to the giant figure. "We can take it from here."

"MANDROID, is there any way we can talk to the soldiers out there?" Arun said from the cockpit.

Yes, there is a loudspeaker system for voice projection.

"Let me do it," said Donna. "You still sound like a kid." She pulled the Dalek voice changer from her backpack.

MANDROID straightened up and took three giant strides towards the huddle of Thorne's men. It levelled both arms at them, taking aim with its cannon.

"You will lay down your arms and surrender immediately," it commanded in a harsh metallic rasp. "You will obey, or

254

be exterminated!"

The cowering men threw their remaining weapons to the ground, shrugged off their grenade belts and raised their trembling hands.

In the Command Bunker, Thorne leaped to his feet and clamped his hands over his ears.

"Aaaaagh! That voice..." he said. "I know that voice!"

"But ... I thought you were Double-X?" Lewis said, looking at Moss, who shrugged.

Saipher had seen enough. "Thorne! You've been outsmarted. It's time to go." Saipher grabbed Thorne's arm and shoved him towards the door. "Start moving! We can still get to the plane!"

The three remaining soldiers grabbed Krishan, Moss and Quinn and bundled them out of the room, hurrying back to the loading dock, past Quinn's agents who were waiting outside.

"Where are you going? What's happening?" Brown shouted as they rushed past.

"Toilet break. You men just stay there and guard the door," Saipher said, leaving them behind.

"MANDROID, are you hurt?" Arun said, looking with concern

at a new schematic on screen, showing MANDROID with some sections blanked out in flashing red.

System damage has been sustained. Self-repair programs are operational. Power levels are at eighty-two per cent.

"What does that mean?" Donna asked. "Can you still kick butt?"

I can ... still ... kick butt.

Sam was tapping away at the keyboard again. "Uh, MANDROID," he said, "do you know who those people are, running from that room at the end?"

They are Professor Krishan Lal, Dr Galahad Thorne and seven others.

"My dad's here?" Arun said, his heart lurching in his chest. "Where are they going?"

Towards the loading bay. They will be on the surface in three minutes.

"We have to stop them. Is there any way we can follow them?"

Yes. Initiating launch sequence now...

Sunny peered through the smashed doors of the barn, the Browning high-power pistol in hand. She checked that no one was there and crept inside.

Several men wearing farm clothes sprawled on the floor. She kneeled beside the nearest and pressed her fingers against his neck to find a pulse, her dark eyes darting around the barn. Her fingers closed on a metal bobble chain round the unconscious man's neck and she saw a pair of small metal plates dangling from it.

"Dog tags?" she said to herself. "Royal Marines – in plain clothes?"

There was a clunk of machinery and a section of the wooden floor began to drop and slide sideways. The lift was coming back up.

"Oh, no," she said.

Sunny snatched a hand grenade from the belt of the unconscious soldier and climbed over a bale of hay for cover, cursing the growing bloom of blood from her left arm. Crouching down, she released the magazine from the handgun and counted the number of bullets. Three. She would have to make them count.

17:38

"Stay right where you are!" Whitby warned, keeping his assault rifle trained on Thorne's defeated troops. The remaining Marines went round, tying the mercenaries' hands behind their backs with their belts.

"Ian, do you feel that?" Burgess said. The hangar floor was vibrating.

Whitby looked up and then felt his legs trembling. "Well, I'll be..." He glanced around in wonder as the hangar walls slowly began to slide into the floor and a split began to widen in the ceiling.

Soon a shaft of daylight streamed into the hangar, glinting off MANDROID's gold trim.

Whitby couldn't help but grin as he breathed in the fresh spring air and saw a glider high overhead. The hangar roof had slid completely aside and the entire floor was lifting, taking Marines, prisoners and the standing vehicle up to the airfield surface.

Sitting inside the MANDROID cockpit and looking up at the

growing square of blue sky, Arun laughed out loud. "This is way cool!" he cried.

The C-130 Hercules was parked at the far edge of the runway, at the end nearest to the barn. The captain had kept the engines running, as instructed, and had lowered the tail ramp.

"This is taking too long," he muttered to himself, while lighting another cigarette. "They should be here by now, with the payload."

"Charlie Echo Bravo Three Four, for the last time, please explain why you are not at the inspection point," squawked a voice from the control tower over the radio.

"Lasham Control, my, uh, brakes seem to have locked. Will be taxiing over shortly, as soon as, uh, the mechanical failure is resolved."

"Charlie Echo Bravo Three Four, this is unacceptable! Please report to—"

"Sorry, Lasham Control, you're breaking up." The captain switched off the radio. "I have to go," he muttered. "I've waited long enough."

Inside the barn, one of Thorne's three soldiers cried out and fell as a bullet caught him in the thigh.

Sunny ducked behind the hay bale again, while the air exploded around her and a barrage of bullets tore through the wooden surround. She held up her compact mirror, tilting it to see what was happening.

The two remaining soldiers were making their way round to flank her, one on each side. Sunny pulled the pin on the grenade with her teeth and held the safety lever down.

Saipher took one look at the situation and sprang into action. Slipping a scalpel from a jacket sleeve, Saipher made swift cuts to remove the cable ties from the ankles of Krishan and Moss.

"This way!" Saipher said, diving for the black Jeep that had earlier smashed its way inside. After yanking the doors open, Saipher shoved Thorne inside, forced Quinn, Krishan and Moss into the back, at knifepoint, and buckled their seat belts. Lewis looked at Thorne, his arms spread wide. "Sorry, no room for baggage!" Saipher said, jumping into the driver's seat, firing up the engine and throwing the gears into reverse.

"Galahad! Wait! After all that I've done for you!" Lewis pleaded, but his voice was lost as Saipher revved the engine and reversed at full speed towards the rear of the barn.

With a bone-jarring smash, the Jeep burst into the daylight amid broken planks and splintering wood.

Thorne's remaining two mercenaries stopped in their tracks to look at the escaping Jeep.

"Catch!" Sunny yelled, popping up from her hiding place and throwing the grenade at the nearest man. He caught it without thinking, then realised what it was and flung it away with a scream of terror. Sunny fired twice, dropping the two men with well-placed shots.

Lewis fell to his knees, hands in the air and face wet with tears. "Please don't shoot me," he blubbed.

Sunny walked over to him, keeping the now empty pistol levelled at him the whole time. She picked up the grenade and slipped it back into her pocket.

"I put the pin back in," she said, seeing the puzzled look on his face. "Now start talking."

Meanwhile, the Hercules had turned to face the runway once more, its pilot pushing forward on the throttles.

"Charlie Echo Bravo Three Four, abort take-off! I repeat, abort take-off! You are not cleared for ascent," said the voice on the radio.

"Sorry, Lasham Control, you'll have to stop me. Over and out," the captain said. He took a last drag on his cigarette, stubbed it out on the instrument panel and released the brake.

The giant aeroplane thundered forward, its four propellers churning the air.

Saipher spun the steering wheel of the Jeep, bringing it round towards the apron of the runway and sped towards the trundling Hercules in front, which was beginning its approach for take-off.

Thorne snatched up his walkie-talkie. "Transport, this is Excalibur. Keep the ramp down. I repeat, keep your ramp down."

"You took long enough," the captain said through the radio. "I almost gave up waiting."

"Just give us enough time to board. Then get the heck out of here."

17:44

Whitby watched the Hercules transport plane lifting into the western skies.

"That's not supposed to be here," he said. "Looks like someone's getting away."

At the wail of sirens he turned to see a convoy of thirty olive-green army vehicles come roaring through the front gates of the airfield: armoured personnel carriers, ambulances, Land Rovers. They turned on to the perimeter road and spread across the runway, speeding towards the Marines and their prisoners.

"And the cavalry's arrived half an hour late," Whitby said.

"At least we can hand over these scumbags," Burgess said, pointing towards Thorne's men. "And then we can get a cold beer."

Whitby nodded. "Amen to that."

Inside MANDROID, Arun was tapping away at the console in front of him, pulling up video feeds from external cameras.

"MANDROID, I can't see where Dad – uh, Professor Lal – is. You said they'd be up top by now."

That is correct. However, Krishan Lal is no longer within sensor range.

"What do you mean? The service lift comes up in the barn, so how far could they get?" Arun couldn't hide the worry creeping into his voice.

Thermal-imaging sensors detect an unusual trajectory.

"Can't this thing speak English?" Donna said.

Plotting reverse thermographic path now.

The front window display changed to show a side elevation view of the airfield, with the barn on the right and the control tower on the left. Arun watched as a thick red-dotted line appeared from the top-left corner and snaked its way diagonally down to the ground. There it changed to a thinner line and crept across the screen to the barn.

Arun frowned. "This is some sort of heat signature, you say? And it's come from the barn and then into the sky? That doesn't make sense."

"It's an aeroplane, you doughnut!" Donna called up. "What else can fly?"

"Uh, we can," Sam said.

"Huh?" Donna and Arun said at the same time.

"I just realised why all those vehicle designs were on the laptop but why we haven't found the rest of the MANDROID fleet," Sam said, his cheeks flushed with excitement. "Because this *is* the fleet."

"Did your mother drop you on your head when you were a baby?" Donna said.

"No, really. Think about it: an all-terrain undetectable vehicle for secret rescue operations. Plus, a whole hangar set aside for only one vehicle?"

Arun pursed his lips. "You know, there's an easy way to tell if Sam is right," he said. "MANDROID, can you fly?" He sniggered, unable to stop himself laughing at how ridiculous the words sounded.

Of course. I have been designed to operate in all environments.

Arun sat upright. "You mean you can *fly*?"

That was your question.

"Did Galahad and my dad get on a plane while we were coming up top?"

That would be a reasonable supposition.

"And can you track the heat signature?"

Yes.

"So what are we waiting down here for? Let's go!"

"Confirmation has come through that an unauthorised transport plane took off from Lasham a few minutes ago," the minister reported to the men seated in the CITADEL boardroom. "We have to assume that the MANDROID device is on board."

"The air strike has been authorised," another official said. "Pilots' orders are to destroy the plane before it reaches international airspace."

"No!" Phelps said in horror.

"I'm sorry. I wish there was another way."

Two RAF Eurofighter Typhoons streaked out of the clouds above Hertfordshire and roared south.

"This is Magpie," one of the pilots said into his radio. "Will be in visual range in approximately two minutes. Over and out."

The convoy of army vehicles had converged on Captain Whitby's unit and hundreds of uniformed soldiers from different regiments were milling about, many stopping to admire the blue and gold metal giant standing in their midst.

"What is that, sarge? Some kind of statue?" a pimply

266

private said, scratching his head and looking at the battered blackened midsection.

"Beats me, but I wouldn't go—"

"Hey, listen up, you lot," a metallic Dalek voice boomed.

"Stone me, it's alive!" the private whispered.

"You need to get your butts out of here, PDQ, as this sucker's about to take off. Otherwise, your behinds are toast."

MANDROID stirred into life, and the troops scattered as a huge leg stepped over their heads and crashed down on to the grass. It walked over to the runway, where it seemed to trip and collapse in on itself. The head and midsection dropped down to re-form the horizontal core. Panels slid out as the sides and rear flattened. The cockpit slid backwards and a pointed cone formed at the front. Finally two tail fins slid upwards.

"There's something you don't see every day," Burgess said.

"Just be glad it's on our side," Whitby said with a smile. "Everyone, keep your heads down!"

With a roar of rocket engines blasting downwards and scorching the runway, MANDROID lifted vertically into the air, hovered as it turned to point west and then disappeared into the sky. The thunderous rumble of its engines rolled over the stunned soldiers as it soared into the blue.

"Plot the shortest route to international airspace," Thorne said to the Hercules pilot. "Once there, we're scot free."

The captain shrugged. "If we head south, we'll be over the English Channel in five minutes."

"Good enough," Thorne said. "Open the ramp in two minutes. I have some rubbish to dispose of."

He ducked back down to the cargo bay where Saipher was sitting on a bulkhead chair, stroking a flare gun. Quinn, Moss and Krishan kneeled opposite, their hands still tied.

Thorne sat beside Saipher and smiled at the faces glaring back.

"Well, well, well," he said, raising his voice above the noise from the engines. "Isn't this cosy? I'll bet none of you expected your day would turn out like this, did you? Me neither." He sighed. "It was such a simple plan: crash a car into Krishan's to steal his laptop, copy over the MANDROID access codes, drive out to the country and then off I go with my creation, ready to deliver to the highest bidder. No one gets hurt. What could go wrong?"

"Why don't you tell me?" growled Quinn.

"A stupid wedding anniversary, that's what. We stage

the crash only to find he doesn't have his laptop with him – the one day all year. So I change plan. The access codes are backed up on his laptop at work, so all we have to do is retrieve it from the safe." Thorne glanced at Saipher. "Simple enough, you would think. I even sent someone to fetch Krishan's son, as extra leverage, but the little runt got away. And then someone else joins the party. Someone who calls himself Double-X."

"You don't say?" Quinn said.

Thorne's voice hardened. "This real Double-X steals Krishan's spare laptop, which I didn't even know he had, copies all the MANDROID data and then – get this – steals the MANDROID himself."

"Yow. Tough break," Quinn said in mock sympathy.

"Which brings me to the reluctant conclusion that the man known as DI Andrew Moss is just that: a London detective in the wrong place at the wrong time."

There was a whirr of hydraulic motors and a roar of rushing air as the cargo ramp began to lower once more.

"The situation is very simple," Thorne said, rising to his feet and shouting to be heard above the wind from the open tail. "While what has transpired today is far from ideal, our position is still salvageable. My backers will, admittedly, not be happy that I have failed to deliver them the MANDROID prototype, but I can give them the next best thing: a full set of plans, plus the brains behind the design."

"I won't help you, Galahad. You know that," Krishan said.

"I think you will. Otherwise, I will just have to ask Saipher here to pay a visit to dearest Heidi and little Arun. Saipher, you can decide how many pieces you wish to bring back."

17:49

"Arun, this might not be the best time to ask, but do you have a plan?" Donna said. "For when we catch up with the plane? I mean, you can't exactly knock on the door and ask if your dad can please come home with you."

Arun's eyes were fixed on the sky ahead, on a tiny dot that was growing larger with each passing second. "We'll think of something," he said. "Worst case, we follow it to wherever it's going and call Sunny to arrange some sort of rescue. I mean, it can't stay in the air forever."

The Hercules was now clearly visible ahead; its squat body and four propellers were unmistakable.

"MANDROID, can they see us?" Arun asked.

Negative. We are making our approach from the target's blind side and are invisible to their instrumentation.

"OK, just get us as close as you can without giving away our position. We need to remain hidden for as long as possible."

"That's Lal, but what about me?" Quinn asked Thorne,

back in the cargo bay of the Hercules.

"You, Mr Quinn, have over thirty years' worth of His Majesty's secrets up here." Thorne tapped the side of his head. "Again, that's worth something. DI Moss, however, has nothing of worth in his head and is, I have to say, literally a waste of space." Thorne snapped his fingers. "Saipher, throw him out."

"No!" Krishan said, trying to stand.

Saipher kicked him in the chest, sending him sprawling, before hauling Moss to his feet and shoving him down the bay to the open ramp at the end.

"Any last requests?" Saipher said, as they stood on the edge of the ramp.

"Yes. Please tell—"

"Ah, who cares?"

Saipher placed a hand on Moss's back, ready to thrust the detective out into the sky.

"Wait!" Thorne said, as his walkie-talkie buzzed.

"Again?" Saipher shrieked.

"Boss, can you come up here?" the pilot called from the cockpit.

"No, I can't," Thorne snapped.

"We've got company."

Thorne ran into the cockpit to see the light grey delta

wings of two Typhoons streak past.

"That's a warning pass," the captain said. "They've been signalling for us to land."

"Never," Thorne said. "How much further till we're safe?"

"A minute, maybe more."

"Then we run for it." He pressed the talk button on his walkie-talkie. "Saipher, put Moss with the others and close the hatch. Then buckle in."

The pilot balked. "We can't outrun those fighters."

"Unless you want to go to jail for a very long time, I'd give it a try."

The Hercules loomed into view once more as MANDROID closed the distance between them.

Arun saw the two fighter jets, one stationed off each wing of the transport plane.

"What's going on?" Arun said. "Are they escorting it down?"

Negative. Transmission intercepts indicate they are issuing final warnings.

"Can we hear them?"

Yes.

"—authorised to shoot you down if you do not accompany us back to base. Raise and lower your flaps to indicate you understand, otherwise you leave us no choice," said the pilot using the call sign Magpie.

Arun immediately looked to the wing flaps. "Go on," he said. "Signal. Signal!"

Nothing happened.

"No more warnings," the pilot said, and the two Typhoons peeled away.

"MANDROID, what's happening?" Arun said.

Their weapon systems are live and targeting is locked.

"Which means what?"

Magpie confirmed target lock on his head-up display and launched one of his AIM-132 heat-seeking air-to-air missiles.

FWOOOOOSSSH! The slim grey missile detached from the wing, its rocket engine fired and it shot towards the Hercules, a vapour trail stretching out behind it.

Arun watched in horror as the missile closed in, ripping into the tail of the Hercules and exploding into a blossom of orange flame. Black smoke streamed from the tail, which partly disintegrated, and the nose of the plane began to drop.

"Dad!" Arun cried as the stricken Hercules fell.

The navigator of the second Typhoon saw a flash of gold in the corner of his eye and looked round in surprise.

"Bogey at five o'clock!" he shouted to the pilot. "It's not showing up on radar."

"That's impossible."

"See for yourself."

The pilot banked the fighter plane and looked over his shoulder.

"No markings," he said.

"Orders are to assume it's hostile."

"Roger that. Prepare to engage."

Commander Lal, be advised that the second Eurofighter has locked its targeting systems on us.

"Dad," Arun said numbly, not hearing as he watched the Hercules drift out of control towards the south coast.

The Typhoon dropped out of the sky behind MANDROID and launched a second missile. The rocket homed in on the heat from the engines and shot towards the blue and gold plane.

17:53

"Arun! Arun!" Donna screamed, pounding her fists on the arm rests. "Argh! Men! MANDROID, get your butt out of here! Now!"

Instruction confirmed.

Donna was slammed into her seat as the MANDROID accelerated once more and turned sharply to the left.

"How ... fast ... can ... you ... go?" Sam said, struggling to speak while being squished into his chair.

Theoretical maximum speed is Mach 10.

"And ... the ... missile...?"

Mach 3.

"Wait..." Arun said, his mind focusing once more. "If ... you ... outrun it ... we'll be ... too far away ... to help ... them..."

"I've got ... an idea!" Donna said. "Slow down... Let it catch up..."

The howl of onrushing air quietened as the engines throttled down.

A graphic display on the front screen showed the positions of the MANDROID and the heat-seeking missile that was homing in on them.

"Now give me a one-eighty-degree turn," Donna said.

Executing now.

"Hang on to your pants!" Donna said, then she squealed in delight as her stomach leaped into her throat.

The MANDROID plane flipped on its nose – one second the cockpit was facing forward, the next it was upside down and looking in the opposite direction. The afterburners fired again and the plane streaked past the oncoming missile.

The missile's on-board computer calculated the change of direction and it looped round in a wide arc, closing in on the MANDROID once more.

The Hercules's pilot pulled up on the yoke with all his strength, straining to prevent the aircraft from going into a spin. There was a rising whine as the plane nosedived.

Behind him, the cargo bay was a scene from hell. Thick black smoke roiled around the ceiling and the back of the plane was on fire.

Saipher was kneeling beside a metal box situated halfway down the bay and was pulling out parachutes. The masked figure stood, pulled one on, over skinny shoulders, and tossed another to Thorne. "Time to go, moron."

"Untie our hands," Quinn said. "There's enough parachutes for all of us."

Saipher turned and threw the five remaining parachutes towards the back of the burning plane. They tumbled over the ragged edge and disappeared. "Oops. Not any more."

Quinn struggled to his feet. "Why, you—"

"Uh-uh," Saipher said, taking aim with the flare gun. "You're going down with the plane, tough guy. Believe me, it's better this way. No witnesses. Thank you for flying Air Einstein."

And with that Saipher took a running jump through the flames at the back of the aeroplane, and out into the sky.

Thorne watched, then looked at Krishan, Moss and Quinn. "The saddest part of all this, Krishan, is that we could both have been rich, were it not for your misguided sense of morality."

Krishan shrugged. "It matters, Galahad. Without anything higher to reach for we're no more than animals."

"Make sure they write that on your gravestone. Here. You can have this back." Thorne took a pocket knife from his jacket and tossed it on the floor by Krishan's feet. "You gave me this for Christmas, eight years ago. Don't look so shocked. I'm not some one-dimensional comic-book villain,

you know. Oh well. Time to cut and run. No pun intended."
Then he ran to the back of the plane and dived out.

Quinn dropped to the floor, rolled on to the knife, opened
the blade and cut the zip tie binding his wrists. He freed
Moss next, then turned to Krishan.

"Just one question," he said as he cut him loose. "How
did you work with that twit for all those years and not
strangle him?"

"MANDROID, take us straight back to whichever plonker
it was who fired that missile at us," Donna said, her eyes
narrowed and nostrils flared.

Following heat signature now.

The MANDROID aircraft shot across the sky, heading
directly towards Magpie.

"Incoming missile on radar!" the Typhoon navigator
called out.

The pilot looked up and saw the MANDROID plane
barrelling towards him, the missile right behind.

"Oh, crud!" he said, pulling up on the joystick, taking the
fighter into a steep climb.

"Perfect!" Donna said. "MANDROID, he's all yours!"

MANDROID's automatic cannon opened fire, sending a
storm of bullets towards the exposed underside of the

Typhoon. The bullets raked the port-side wing, shredding the metal as if it were tissue paper. The wing fell away and the body of the plane spun out of control.

"Go for the wing!" Donna cried.

MANDROID twisted in mid-air and dived after the falling wing, plunging through the column of smoke trailing from the Hercules.

The heat-seeking missile changed direction and shot after the blue and gold plane.

The loose wing loomed large in the cockpit window as MANDROID caught up with it before a second burst of cannon fire shredded it into a cloud of fragments.

MANDROID rolled and flew through the cloud. The missile followed, slammed into a chunk of falling debris and exploded into a fireball.

Donna whooped. "Bullseye! That's how you do it!"

Why did you not deploy chaff cartridges? the AI said. *I am fully equipped with missile countermeasure systems including infrared flares and active decoys.*

"Now you tell me!"

"MANDROID, can you confirm that the crew ejected safely?" Arun asked.

Sensors detect four parachutes in the air.

"Four? Not two?"

"Maybe some skydivers?" Sam offered.

"No time to worry about that. How long before that plane hits?"

If it maintains its current glide pattern, ninety-three seconds.

Inside the Hercules cockpit, the captain and Quinn were pulling back on one steering column, Krishan and Moss on the other.

An undulating carpet of green – the hills of the West Sussex Downs – spread out below the plummeting plane. Beyond lay the sparkling sea.

"We're going to crash!" Moss cried.

"No ... we ... are ... not," the captain said through clenched teeth, pulling back as hard as he could. The veins on his neck stood out like cords.

A group of hikers on the limestone cliffs of West Sussex looked up at the falling plane screaming towards them and scattered, along with a flock of sheep, running for cover.

The stricken plane plunged towards the clifftop. Its shadow flew across the grass, the outline becoming sharper as the aeroplane neared the ground.

"We're not going to make it!" Moss screamed.

"Hold on!" the captain cried.

The underside of the heavy plane drew closer to the cliff edge and struck it. There was a tremendous grinding sound and a groan from the shuddering airframe as the Hercules scraped the cliff, sending an avalanche of broken chalk rumbling down to the rocks below.

"That was too close," the captain said.

"Can we make a water landing?" Krishan asked.

"Not with an uncontrolled descent. If we go in too fast, at the wrong angle, it'll be like hitting concrete."

"At least we'll not be hitting civilians," Quinn muttered.

MANDROID roared out of the sky, closing in on the Hercules.

Crash-landing in seventy-seven seconds.

"I have a question," Sam said. "What happened to the other—"

The second Typhoon dived out of a thick cloud bank and launched all four of its ASRAAM missiles at the MANDROID.

The window display changed to show four red dots converging.

"Just what we don't need right now," Arun said.

Crash-landing in sixty-five seconds.

"MANDROID, deal with the incoming missiles any way you want," Arun said. "Just get us to the plane before it hits."

Instruction confirmed.

Panels on the MANDROID wings slid aside and the automatic cannon deployed. Their mountings pivoted and they turned to face backwards.

The four missiles streaked closer, their contrails twisting together in braids.

The autocannon let loose with a thundering hail of bullets, smashing the missiles out of the sky. One of them exploded, its shockwave triggering another fireball. The guns pivoted again, this time switching aim to the watching Typhoon. A second blast of automatic fire rained upwards.

Banking sharply, the fighter jet accelerated away, into the shadow of the cliff face. The autocannon tracked its path and strafed the cliff ahead, blasting huge chunks of chalk into its way. The Typhoon swerved and tried to pull up but there was no time: a large rock smashed on to the wing, flipping the plane.

The cockpit canopy fizzed and jettisoned as two ejector seats launched, throwing both pilot and navigator clear.

The Typhoon, its wing crippled, spun and slammed into

the cliff face, exploding into fiery fragments.

"Nice shooting!" Donna said.

Crash-landing in forty-eight seconds.

"Sam, talk to me!" Arun said. "The plane's going in too fast and too steep. It's never going to make it."

Sam was tapping on the keyboard. "Uh, it's the loss of the tail that's causing the sharp angle of descent. The speed is the lesser problem. Sort out the tail and you sort out the speed."

"MANDROID, this is going to sound crazy, but hear me out, OK?" Arun said. "Can you somehow configure yourself to form a tail?"

All current configurations are vehicular in nature. While it may be theoretically poss—

"My gosh, it sounds like you!" Donna said. "Yes or no, tin head?"

Yes.

"Then do it!"

The Hercules pilot swore as he saw the grey-black waves of the English Channel shimmering below. The sea looked glassy and calm but he knew that meant nothing. Hitting it, even at a reduced speed of 120 knots, would still smash the plane to pieces.

"There's nothing more I can do," he said, exhausted. "I'm sorry."

"Brace yourselves!" Quinn said, knowing it was a worthless comment. He strapped himself into a pull-down seat behind the captain.

Suddenly a shadow flashed across the cockpit, accompanied by a roar of overhead thunder.

Krishan looked up immediately, eyes wide. "I know that sound," he said, running back to the cargo bay.

"Wait, what are you doing?" Moss shouted after him.

The MANDROID plane drew up alongside the shattered tail. Its wings slid inwards and thickened to form arm-like columns.

Crash-landing in twelve seconds.

"Just keep your mind on the job!" Arun said.

The arms reached out and clamped themselves on to the Hercules fuselage, where the shattered base of the tail joined the main body of the plane. The blue and gold rear section started to extend and flatten.

Krishan stood by the cockpit door and laughed out loud as he watched what was happening. "Whoever would have thought it could do that?" he said.

* * *

Crash-landing in eight seconds.

"MANDROID, watch the wing flaps and match their angles! We need maximum lift to level the plane," Arun said.

"It's working!" Sam said.

Crash-landing in four seconds... Three... Two...

The Hercules glided majestically towards the onrushing sea like a wounded eagle. Its body was dull grey but the tail was a resplendent blue and gold, which guided it down and brought it in parallel to the sea.

The undercarriage hit first, waves clutching at the belly of the plane and pulling at it, sending it slewing sideways. The propeller blades chewed the water and shattered, sending shards flying. The airframe groaned and interior metal beams buckled. The tail section, to which the MANDROID was clinging, broke away completely, sending the blue and gold figure hurtling forward to smash through the starboard wing and to tumble head over tail, like a toy thrown in a tantrum.

Inside the MANDROID, cartwheeling over the sea, Arun, Sam and Donna screamed as one before they blacked out.

The Hercules rolled on to its side, its intact wing rising like the fin of a humpback whale before it flopped down again and started to sink.

Inside the cockpit, the water was already waist deep. Quinn grabbed a fire extinguisher and smashed the remaining windows.

"Everybody out!" he bellowed, shooing Moss and the pilot onwards. He looked around. "Krishan! Lal! Where are you?"

The water was now up to his shoulders. Quinn cursed and plunged back into the cargo bay to find a body floating near the cockpit door.

"Krishan!" Quinn grabbed for him, turned him over and saw a fresh cut on his forehead staining the water red. "Why does nobody ever listen to me?" Quinn grumbled.

He took a deep breath, pulled Krishan to the cockpit and out through the window, swimming as hard as he could away from the plane before it slipped beneath the waves and was gone.

In the CITADEL boardroom, the sense of relief was palpable.

General McAllister pulled a hip flask from his pocket and took a long gulp of whisky before passing it round.

"Gentlemen, I am glad to report the crisis is over," the minister said. "Latest reports are that both this MANDROID device and the transport plane have been destroyed. We should all remember that we have lost some very fine people today—"

"Not to mention hundreds of millions of pounds of taxpayer money," another official added.

"But the security threat to our nation is over. I think it's safe to say we have seen the last of this MANDROID business and that we can all congratulate ourselves on a job well done."

"Hear, hear," echoed the suits in the room.

McAllister looked unconvinced.

19:33

"Ow, my head," Arun said, opening his eyes.

He was in near darkness. Only the soft glow of LEDs and instrument panels told him where he was. "Sam? Donna?"

They are both unconscious. Donna will awaken in approximately twelve minutes, Sam in seventeen. Both are well and vital signs are good.

"What happened?"

The tail section broke loose from the fuselage. Momentum threw us clear and system damage was sustained.

"You're hurt? How badly?"

Self-repair programs are operational. Power levels are at nineteen per cent.

"Can you get us home?"

Yes.

Arun looked at his watch. "Hey, if it's only half past seven, why is it so dark outside?"

A flash of silver swam up to the window and a fish stopped to nibble at the glass.

"You turned into a ... submarine?"

Yes.

"This has been a very weird, very long day. Um, MANDROID?"

Yes?

"Do you know if my dad...?"

Projected outcomes based upon speed and trajectory of the damaged aircraft are all positive.

"We did it?"

We did it.

Arun smiled a smile so wide that his cheeks ached. Then he started to cry, great wracking sobs that shook his slim body as he released all the strain and tension he had been carrying knotted up inside him during the day.

When he finally stopped blubbing, he wiped his eyes on his grubby sleeve and asked, "Are there people up there still looking for you?"

Yes.

"I have an idea how we can get you home without being seen. First, can you get rid of the bomb – you know, disable it and dump it on the seabed – and then plot us a course up the Thames to Kew?"

21:46

MANDROID, now in motorised caravan mode, parked in the corner of a builders' yard.

The battered side door opened and Donna, Sam and Arun crept out.

"Goodnight, MANDROID," Arun said, patting the metal. He turned to his friends. "So we're agreed?"

Sam nodded. "Oh, yeah!"

Donna smiled. "Sure. This isn't stealing – it's finders keepers. Besides, I think everyone else proved they can't be trusted with this thing."

"Does that include me?" a voice said from the shadows.

The children jumped and made ready to run.

"Hold it! I'm not telling anyone anything," the voice said.

"Mossy?" Donna said, her nose wrinkling.

"That's Detective Inspector Moss to you," Moss said, and stepped out into the glare of a security lamp.

"How much trouble are we in?"

"That depends on how the next ten minutes go. Come with me. I have someone who's been dying to meet you."

Donna looked to Sam and Arun for guidance but the boys shrugged. She sighed and they followed Moss out of the yard to a waiting black Range Rover.

"In you go," Moss said, opening the rear door and ushering them in, before climbing into the driver's seat.

Inside, a stocky grey-haired man was waiting.

"We meet at last," he said.

"I know you," Arun said, recognising the voice. "Mr Quinn, from MI6? You were at my house this morning."

"Clever boy. Your dad did mention that about fifty times," Quinn said.

"You've seen Dad?" Arun said, eyes wide. "How is he?"

"Well, considering he's been in a car crash, had a beating, a spot of torture, a near drowning and a plane crash, he's doing remarkably well. Keeps asking if Newcastle beat Arsenal, though, in tonight's match, so there might be some brain damage." He smiled. "I'm taking you to see him."

"Where is he?"

"At West Middlesex Hospital. Don't worry, he's fine. He's in for observation. Your mum's there, by his side, and I've got Patel in the next room. Moss, do the honours, please."

Moss started the car and headed north.

"First things first," Quinn said, looking at the three worried faces, "you're not in any trouble, not with the authorities at least. I can't speak for your parents who will probably ground you as your reward for saving the world."

"What have you told them?" Donna asked.

"You three bunked off school and went to the flicks. I have ticket stubs to prove it, plus Pizza Hut and bowling receipts."

Donna's mouth fell open.

"Listen, only a handful of people know what really happened today and most of them are in this car," Quinn said. "You may not realise it, but you've saved millions of lives, including mine. You kids are clever, you're brave, you're resourceful. If you were older, I'd offer you a job."

Arun's cheeks burned. "So can we keep it?" he asked.

"How does this sound to you? This MANDROID thing was never meant to be a weapon. Your father designed it for search and rescue before Whitehall messed with it. So how about we leave it where it is for safekeeping, and if it's ever needed for rescue operations, I'll give you a call? Looks to me like you know how to use it. No one's going to find it since it's undetectable, and I doubt you're going to be taking it in to 'show-and-tell'. What do you say?"

"Is there a catch?" Donna asked.

"No catch. I owe you my life."

She grinned. "Totally wicked, man! We're in!" She high-fived Arun and then Sam, whose hand stung afterwards.

"Two things, Mr Quinn," Arun said.

"Go on."

"What happened to Galahad?"

Quinn turned away for a moment, darkness falling over his face. "I won't lie to you. He got away. Him and the other character. We've alerted Interpol and he's on Europe's most wanted list. It's only a matter of time, but we'll get him. What's the other question?"

"Why trust us with this thing, after all the money it cost to build?"

"Because you have integrity. You won't abuse it and you won't be tempted to sell it for cash, unlike most other people I know."

Donna burst out laughing. "Oh, man, I like you! You are so full of it! What's the real reason?"

Quinn smiled. "Because no one would ever suspect you of doing what you've done. You're just kids."

"Yeah, I know," Sam said. "Sick, isn't it?"

"If we're going to help you, but we can't talk about any of this, we're going to need code names, right?" Arun said. "And secure comms."

"I've already thought of that," Quinn said. "Your team name is *STEALTH*."

"Oh, that is way cool!" Sam blurted.

Donna nodded her approval. "That'll work."

"What does it stand for?" Arun said. "It must mean something."

"It does. I'll tell you later."

"And what about us?" Sam asked. "We'll need code names too. You can't use our real names."

Quinn put both hands over his face. "I don't need this right now. I've had a long day."

"Come on, you have to," Sam insisted. "You owe us. You said so."

"Fine. OK." He pointed at Sam. "You, you're Baby." He turned to Arun. "You're Ginger."

Quinn leaned towards Donna who glared at him.

"Don't you dare—" she started.

"Posh. If you don't like them, you can change them later."

"Too right," Sam said. "And what should we call you?"

"I know," Arun said. "We'll call you Old Spice, since you've just named us after the Spice Girls and you're obviously old."

"And they wonder why I hate kids," Quinn muttered to himself.

22:04

"Dad!" Arun cried and threw his arms round his father, who was sitting up in the hospital bed.

"Easy on the ribs, son. They're a bit bruised." He grinned and mussed up Arun's hair.

Sam and Donna crept into the private room, while Quinn waited outside.

Heidi took a firm grip on Arun's filthy shirt collar and pulled him aside.

"What's this I've been hearing about you skipping school all day?" she hissed. "And look at the state of your clothes."

"Mum," Arun said, "you're embarrassing me."

"You've all had me worried sick." Heidi cast an appraising eye over Donna before fixing her icy stare on Sam. "I expect better from you. That's it, no more game time for you two. Arun's banned for a month."

"Mum, that's not fair," Arun said.

"Keep arguing and it'll be two months."

"Go easy on him, dear," Krishan said. "Everyone deserves a break now and then. Let's just be grateful we're all back safely. What film did you kids see that was worth missing school for?"

"*Fast and Furious Twelve*," Donna said without missing a beat.

"Is that the one where they save the plane from crashing?" A faint smile played on Krishan's lips.

"Nah," Donna said. "That was the previous one."

"When the secret weapon gets destroyed?"

She held his gaze. "And no one ever talks about it again."

"That's the one," Krishan said. "You think they're done with all that?"

Donna smiled. "I'd say they're only just getting started."